AND A MEADOWLARK SANG

Jen Pretty

I have been bent and broken, but — I hope- into a better shape.

—CHARLES DICKENS, GREAT EXPECTATIONS

CHAPTER ONE

You know what's crazy? Vampires. Ya. They are crazy sonsabitches. Always lurking about in the dark and then popping up and biting people. You should think about it.

This isn't about vampires though. It's about me. And I'm not a vampire. I'm just a consistently poor, minimum-wage overnight employee of the twenty-four-hour Discount Emporium. I also have an unhealthy interest in the undead because of a tiny problem I've had since I was a little girl. We'll get to that in a minute though. I have bigger issues than paying the rent on the ridiculous one-room hovel that my absentee landlord calls an apartment.

Thankfully, the clock said I only had one hour left in my shift. My old black combat boots were killing my feet, and I hadn't had a coffee since the start of my shift eight hours ago.

"Did you find everything you were looking for?" I asked, giving the lady with three screaming kids a tight smile. She ignored me and grabbed one of her wayward children before the little dearie smashed his sibling over the head with a cereal box. She loaded all her purchases on the small counter, and I dutifully scanned the items. With her distracted, the children got away from her and started destroying the display of Pringles my boss had me construct at the start of my shift.

The violent boy child who was previously wielding the cereal box now had a Pringles can in each hand and shook them, maraca style, dangerously close to his sibling's head. The younger child started screaming and ran back to his mother's side, knocking a stack of batteries off a shelf in his haste. I tried hard to like children, but until they could act like humans instead of rabid animals, I was out.

"That will be fourteen seventy," I said trying not to let annoyance show on my face.

She handed me a twenty-dollar bill while reprimanding her oldest child and trying to get her still crying child into the cart amongst the baby in a carrier and the shopping bags.

When they were finally out of the store, I sighed and started straightening the disaster left in their wake. I told myself busy work made the time go faster, but my brain knew better. When my shift finally ended and the elderly woman who worked mornings shuffled in, I went to the break room, collected my wallet, cell, and keys, and then hustled out hoping to sneak past my boss's office.

"Can I speak to you a minute before you go, Lark?" my boss, Mr. Fellum, said in his deep baritone voice.

Crap. He always smelled bad. The schedule was in the break room, and there was no earthly reason for this weekly recitation of my shifts. He seemed to think I was irresponsible, or maybe he just thought I was stupid. I'm not. Stupid, I mean. I'm not irresponsible either, but the fact that I was quiet, and petite made people think I needed my handheld and the crust cut off my sandwich. I dutifully took a half step into the tiny closet he called an office and stood awkwardly waiting for him to speak.

"Have a seat. I'll go over your schedule with you," he said like he did every Friday. I found if I put the dates into my phone while I was in front of him, he would leave me alone until the next Friday. I got out my phone and sat in the hard-plastic chair across the cluttered desk from Mr. Smellum - I mean Fellum.

"I have you down for Monday, Wednesday and Thursday," He said trying to straighten some of the papers on his desk and failing to put a dent in the mess.

I typed madly on my phone, so it would be convincing that I was putting it down. I always worked overnight Monday, Wednesday, and Thursday, so remembering was not a stretch of my mental capacity, but he's the boss.

In all honesty, I was sending a text to my neighbour Frankie, reminding him we were going out tonight. As soon as

I sent the short text, I got a confirmation reply, my phone on silent so my boss wouldn't know, I smiled up at him to let him know I had dutifully put that critical information into my phone.

He smiled back and leaned forward on his desk. The smell of cheap cologne and cigarette smoke clogged my nose before he said, "That's great, Lark. I'll see you Monday night, then."

I stood and pocketed my phone, muttered a thanks would not do anything to increase his faith in me and headed out the door.

I was used to being thought of as slow, so I tried just to let that go. I had no close relationships or family, and it was better that way.

I am a master at keeping secrets, and I have plenty of them to keep.

I made it to my car and unlocked the door. It wasn't a great neighbourhood, but, my old Honda was nearly rusted through and wasn't attractive enough for any of the local thugs to be bothered stealing.

The sun was just peeking over the horizon between the buildings. This was my favourite time of day - before the people started filling the streets. The sun was for other people, not for me. I was born for the night and always struggled to keep my eyes open during the day. One of the families I had lived with cared enough to have me checked for some kind of sleep disorder. There was nothing wrong with me. I just slept during the day and stayed up all night. School was a disaster for me, and I only managed to graduate because I finished my last year online. At night.

My car started on the second try, and I drove across the city. It took me almost a year of taking the bus and saving every penny to buy the car, but I couldn't afford to keep it unless I lived in the tiny shoebox apartment across town, so it really wasn't the saving grace I thought it would be. I wanted to put some roots down here, though. The city was beautiful, in places, and the crowds big enough I could hide. So, I made every effort to carve out a life that I could see myself living.

I pulled into my parking space at the back of the brick turn-of-the-century house that had been converted to eight small apartments. Mine, the smallest, was on the top floor. It was really an attic crawlspace, but luckily my diminutive five feet allowed me to stand up in the middle. Probably the only benefit to being short.

The morning sun streamed through the open blinds of my apartment as I dropped my keys in the bowl by the door and walked into the tiny kitchen. I flicked on the stereo to cover the sound of the Petersons fighting on the floor below and took out a frozen dinner. It didn't matter that it was seven am, it was dinnertime for me. I popped it in the microwave and closed the window blinds. The darkness of my apartment was soothing after a full night in fluorescent lighting.

Once I'd finished my dinner and washed my fork, I changed into pyjamas and collapsed into bed to sleep till it was time to head out with Frankie.

My eyes peeled open slowly and checked the clock. It was already four in the afternoon and time to get moving if I wanted to eat and get dressed before Frankie banged down my door. I hopped into my tiny shower and scrubbed the sleep out of my eyes. My black, shoulder length hair was low maintenance so, when I was done, I dried it quickly, checked my pale complexion in the mirror, sighed, wrapped myself in my favourite robe, and made breakfast while watching the news. There were three more missing people. In a city of only two hundred thousand people, there were a lot of missing people. More than the national average. Enough to be noticeable but not enough to cause a panic or bring too much attention to the city. Most people brushed it off, but I knew the truth. The dark underbelly of any given city was well hidden from the ordinary folks who went about their daily lives in peace.

Until their peace was ruined.

I clicked off the TV and dressed quickly in my favourite black jeans and a black tank top with a bit of lace along the top. Ya, I'm a bit cliché, so what? The bars in the area were dark and not too loud, that's where Frankie and I always headed.

Frankie and I had similar life goals. Goal one was to stay out of our shitty apartments as much as possible. Frankie lived below the Peterson's who lived below me. The Petersons' screaming matches were legendary. Mrs. Peterson's voice was so high pitched I sometimes wondered how the windows hadn't shattered, and Mr. Peterson tended to throw things. Breakable things.

Goal two was to keep our friendship low key. Frankie was good looking, but I never felt any real chemistry between us. I wasn't sure Frankie was even interested in women. In truth, we didn't know much more about each other than names and cell numbers. That worked for me. Plus, company in my free time was nice. He was just coming off his job at whatever he did as I was getting up for the night. I had never asked him what he did. It didn't matter.

About fifteen minutes later there was a bang on my door. The Petersons were getting wound up, so Frankie's timing was perfect

I opened the door while fishing my keys out of the bowl and he spun on his heel. I followed behind in silence. Frankie was average height with dark, near black hair that flopped over his forehead. He always wore the same leather jacket with 'Crossroads' scrolled across the back. I assumed it was a gang or motorcycle club. I had never seen another jacket like it. We walked a few blocks up the road to Arnie's Bar and Grill. Arnie's was mostly a sports bar. Big TV's mounted on the walls displayed the latest football game recaps, and the music was on. A handful of men in jerseys were sitting around drinking beers, but it was otherwise empty. It was still early.

Frankie and I chose our seats, one between us so we didn't have to sit so close, and we ordered drinks. I always had gin and tonic, and he always had rum and coke. We spent more than an hour enjoying that peace.

"Come here often?"

Just like that my peace was broken by a slurring, drunk, jersey-wearing idiot. Fuck me. Usually, Frankie's presence kept the riff-raff away. On special nights, though, a drunk guy would take it in his head to approach me.

I spoke without turning my head. "Not interested."

"How can you know if you haven't even looked at me?" he muttered and stumbled onto the seat beside me.

I prayed for strength and then turned my head and caught sight of him. His head was tipped back like it might fall off his shoulders and his eyes half closed. He was just about to pass out. Not a catch. I looked him in the eye and deadpanned, "Not interested."

That didn't go over well. He stumbled off his bar stool and narrowed his eyes. "You dumb bitch. You are lucky to get my attention. Do you even know who I am?"

"Alright, Ted, back off or I'll have to ask you to leave," Arnie said from behind the bar where he had been wiping the perfectly clean bar top in stereotypical bartender manner.

"Fine," the drunk man muttered. "I'm leaving, anyway." Then he staggered out the door and into the night.

I threw back my drink and ordered another. Frankie caught my eye and gave me a wink before he set down his glass and headed to the washrooms in the back.

"You Ok?" a refined voice asked from the seat drunk Ted had vacated.

I couldn't catch a break. I took another big gulp of my drink before I spoke. At least this one didn't sound drunk.

"I'm fine," I answered curtly, hoping he could take a hint.

He couldn't.

"Do you often attract the disgustingly inebriated?" he asked, giving the bartender a wave. My heart rate spiked as I caught a glimpse of him from the corner of my eye, unwilling to give him my complete attention but also immediately sure I never wanted to turn my back on him either.

"You don't appear disgustingly inebriated," I mimicked, trying to act natural. "So, I guess not always."

See this is where my problem came in. I knew the man beside me was dead. As far as I could tell, I was the only one who knew. I had never met anyone else who mentioned this unmarketable skill, but then, advertising it was apparently akin to a death wish.

The first time I remember commenting on a person being a vampire, I was only eight, and the ensuing bloodbath left me barely alive and an orphan. Not a mistake one repeats.

I bravely turned my back to the vamp to watch Frankie saunter down the hall. I finished my drink quickly before peeking back at the stool beside me. It was now vacant. I breathed a sigh of relief. I did not need that kind of stress in my life.

I had assumed, after my first encounter with a vampire, that being able to identify the vamps made me an instant threat and target. No reason to test the theory and no need to tempt fate by hanging around one.

By midnight Frankie was toast, and I was tipsy, so we walked our sorry asses' home and said goodnight. It was more of a grunt and a wave, but the sentiment was there.

It was only about two in the morning, so I surfed the net for a while and then turned on a movie and settled down to watch. At around five thirty Saturday morning I headed out to the gym. I taught yoga for beginners twice a week and took an advanced yoga class every other day. My therapist recommended yoga to one of my foster families when I was a preteen. It became my sacred place of peace; the first place I could go to be near other people without the need to interact beyond trivial small talk. This morning was my kid's class. They were mostly twelve to fifteen-year-olds who were into competitive sports, and their coaches used yoga for cross training. It was a fun, easy class with well-behaved and disciplined kids.

The rewards of teaching the kids were not lost on me. I enjoyed their enthusiasm and energy. It was the exact opposite of everything else in my life, and I didn't squander it.

"Hi Lark!" one of the girls from the Hockey team said. I had four hockey girls in my class, and they were all diligent and polite – a product of the highly competitive local sports teams that consistently developed national level players.

I smiled, one of my first honest smiles this week, and waved back before strolling to the change rooms to lock up my stuff and get ready for class.

It was a full class, including a few new kids. They worked hard, and we focused on breathing with some small exercises they could practice at home, and I demonstrated some new positions we would be working on over the rest of the month. By the time my class was over, I felt relaxed and supple. The stretching always helped focus my mind, and the exercise calmed my body.

A horde of sweaty teens wandered off to the change rooms, and I headed to the weight room to work on my upper body strength for a while. My advanced yoga class demanded much more strength and control than the basic classes, and I was lacking in that department. With my goal of eventually owning my own yoga studio, I felt compelled to work hard now, even though it was all a pipe dream. My chances of ever being able to pay rent on a studio were zero, but I kept my focus on the dream I had been chasing since my teenage years.

Clearly, I should have been focusing on my surroundings too because when a throat cleared behind me, I turned and found myself face to face with not one, but two vampires and they were staring at me.

CHAPTER TWO

Now, I don't believe in coincidences, and I had never seen more than one vamp in a month, so seeing three in twenty-four hours meant very bad news for me.

Be cool.

"Hey, how's it going?" I muttered, pretending they weren't blood-sucking monsters.

Their jeans and heavy boots made it obvious they weren't here to work on their fitness, but I could pretend not to notice that too. I moved across the room, keeping them in my peripheral vision, trying to get enough space between us that it didn't seem odd when I turned for the door. Unfortunately, they stayed between me and the only exit.

That's when I knew I was screwed. I quit the act and made a mad dash for the door. Before I got two steps, they were in front of me. I bounced off one of them, and landed on my ass, with the wind knocked out of me. I wished I had thought to scream before I ran because there was no chance of screaming now.

As I gasped, one of the vampires crouched in front of me and held up a white business card with small plain type. He flashed his fangs at me, then set the card on the floor by my feet, stood up and dusted his jacket like I had sullied it by smashing into him. They both turned and left without having spoken a single word.

I heard the gym door close, and finally got half a lung full of air so put it to use racing for the lady's locker room. Thankfully everyone from the morning classes had cleared out. I flicked the lock and slid down to the hard floor, resting my cheek on the cool door.

They hadn't killed me. Yet.

After about ten minutes of deep breathing, I remembered the card. I gave myself a serious pep talk and cracked the locker room door open. No one was around, so I crept back to the weight room and snatched the card off the ground before returning and relocking the door.

The card displayed an address on the expensive side of town. On the back was today's date and 9 pm scribbled in pen. The threat was obvious, and the invitation didn't seem optional, but who the hell shows up to their own death sentence? That would be a big nope from me.

When my legs felt steady again, I changed and went home, looking over my shoulder every five seconds to make sure they weren't following me. I locked my door, and double checked the window locks, then had a quick shower that left some shampoo in my hair, but I didn't care. I couldn't hear shit with the shower running.

I tossed on some clothes and grabbed a steak knife from my kitchen before double checking the locks. I tucked the knife under my pillow and laid down to stare at the ceiling for the next eight hours. Having received death threats from monsters, I wasn't about to have a nice nap.

By 5 PM. I was wired and exhausted. My eyelids were heavy, and my stomach was roiling. My mind kept spinning around the same thoughts. If they knew where I lived, I had to leave. If I left my apartment, I was a sitting duck, but I couldn't stay here if they knew where I lived. I had about a hundred dollars in my bank account. That would fill my tank a few times. I could probably get pretty far on a couple of tanks of gas.

Decision made, I packed a few of my most important belongings and some clothes into a suitcase and filled another bag with food. I had already bought food for the week. I wouldn't waste it.

I carried my two measly bags down the stairs and out to the parking lot. My parking space turned out to be empty. I apparently no longer had a car.

In its place was another card with the words 'we have your car' scribbled on it.

They knew where I lived and had stolen my car? Were they here now, watching me? Could they stand around in the daylight? The two vamps from the gym must have been able to walk in sunlight. There were no accurate sources for information on vampires. I should know. I had spent most of my life searching. All I could find was folklore and fiction.

In case they were watching me, I walked back into my building with my bags. It was almost 6 pm now, so I still had three hours to kill before the deadline. Think Lark! Argh.

I grimaced and leaned against the door when I got back in the safety of my apartment. I could hitchhike or get a bus ticket if I could get out of here without them seeing me, the only problem was I couldn't tell if someone was watching from the midday shadows.

Screw it.

I pulled out my phone and sent a text to Frankie: I need to get out of here.

Maybe I could lose them if I was out somewhere busy and crowded.

His reply was almost instant: Meet you downstairs.

Thank God.

I couldn't take my bags, but maybe I'd get away with my life.

I stumbled down the last few stairs. Luckily Frankie's hand caught my arm and righted me. Taking the lead, he walked away from our building. I looked around nervously trying to catch sight of the vampires but couldn't see anyone following us. Frankie glanced at me a couple of times like he knew something was up. I probably looked like I'd been through a hurricane. That's how the last 12 hours felt. The farther we walked, the more my heart rate slowed and the more convinced I became that we weren't being followed at all.

Eventually, Frankie turned into an alley and did some fancy knock on an unmarked door.

The door swung open, and Frankie walked in. As he moved away from the door, I could see it was a dimly lit, empty warehouse. The door stood open in front of me, waiting for my decision. We had never been here before. I could hear music coming from somewhere inside, but it was faint like there were a few other doors between me and the sound. Before I could make my own decision about entering the creepy place, Frankie's arm slinked out, grabbed my wrist, and pulled me in. The door slammed shut behind me. I have excellent night vision, always have had. Still, it took a second for my eyes to adjust. When they did, I couldn't believe what I saw.

The walls of the vast space were painted with faded and chipped murals of battlefields, largely consisting of men with swords, and dragons diving from the sky. In fact, when I looked up, the whole ceiling seemed to be covered in time-faded dragons of various colours moving through the oily sky like thunderclouds.

"What the hell?" I asked Frankie. He knew exactly what I meant. This wasn't a bar. He was holding a bottle of rum though, so this place almost fit the bill. There was a man with a bored expression sitting beside the door we had come through. He wasn't paying us any attention though. He had headphones on and seemed to be watching videos on his phone.

Frankie cleared his throat. "You're safe here," was all he said.

Did he know? Oh crap. My receding panic shot back through the roof.

I whispered, "Safe from what?" He had to say it first: I didn't want to say it. Frankie and I didn't talk about our stuff. We didn't know things about each other. Maybe it was just Frankie who was a mystery and somehow, in the last year, hanging out with him, I had somehow blabbed all my secrets.

He just thrust the bottle of rum into my hands. I stared at him for a moment, but he didn't seem inclined to answer me. So, I took a sip and let the rum burn all the way down my throat. I had never liked rum, but this was one of those moments when hard alcohol was necessary.

Frankie walked over to the far side of the open space and sat on a lumpy couch, so I followed him and sat down too. That's what we always did. He walked somewhere, and I just followed along. It had occurred to me before now, but at that moment it became clear that I trusted Frankie for no other reason than I trusted him. I didn't know him really. He had just become a solid anchor I could cling to without all the usual requirements of friendship.

I drank some more to try and delay the inevitable. He knew. I knew that he knew. I didn't know how he knew, but I was sure he did. He wouldn't have brought me to this place and told me it was safe for no reason.

I peeked at him out of the corner of my eye, but his head was tipped back, resting on the back of the couch, eyes closed. This sucked. Our unspoken pact was going to be ruined. Wasn't my whole life in the toilet now anyway? The vampires knew where I lived. They had found me at my gym. They had my piece-of-shit car.

"Vampires," I said as a tear tried to creep out.

He lifted his head, nodded once and rested his head back down -- never even opening his eyes

That was that. I had always assumed I wasn't the only person who knew about vampires but finding out Frankie knew made me feel closer to him. I took another swig from the bottle and wiped my eyes. I still felt restless. Frankie said it was safe here but how long could I stay holed up in this building? I didn't want to ask questions. Asking always led to being asked and answering led to death and destruction.

"I need to get out of town," I said, hugging the nearly empty bottle of alcohol.

He rolled his head to the side, looking directly at me. "You can't. It's too late," he muttered unhappily.

I stood up suddenly. "What do you mean it's too late?" I asked, bewildered.

He muttered under his breath and then cleared his throat. "They won't let you leave. You got a card, you go. There is no point in trying to fight it. How much time do you have?"

I checked my phone and another hour had passed since I discovered my car missing. "Two hours," I said before turning away and pacing across the room and back again. "I can't go there." I was going to pass out if I didn't calm my breathing. My vision was narrowing. I took a deep breath and centred myself.

Frankie rose to stand beside me. That had been the most we had spoken to each other in the year we had lived in the same building. The first night I moved in, we sat beside each other at the bar around the corner until we both got kicked out at closing time. We stumbled home, sort of together. Mostly me following along behind him trying to make it look like we were together so the thugs on the corner wouldn't bother me.

I closed my eyes and rubbed my forehead, pushing away the memory. When I opened my eyes again, things were blurry, the edges of my vision hazy.

"Sit down a minute, Lark," he said. It was the first time he used my name, and it pulled me back from the encroaching darkness. I collapsed on the couch and put my head between my knees, forcing my breathing to slow.

This was just great. I was probably going to pass out, and the vampires would find me here and kill me.

"They probably won't kill you," he responded like he could hear my thoughts.

I tried to look at him, but my head spun as soon as I sat up, so I leaned back down and took a few deep breaths before I spoke. "How do you know?"

I chanced a peek at him, but he was just sitting there staring blankly at the wall. After another moment, he finally spoke again, "I just know. You'll have to trust me."

That was the kicker. I did trust him. What kind of person trusted someone they had never had a conversation with? I didn't even know his last name.

"It's Thompson," he muttered.

"What's Thompson?" I asked still breathing in through my nose and out through my mouth in an exaggerated way.

"That's my last name."

I sat up, and the room spun. "What? I... Did you just read my mind?"

"We each have our gifts," he muttered, waving the question away like it was inconsequential. "I had hoped you could stay in the human world longer, but I guess your time is up. You have to go talk to Mr. Crowden."

"Who is Mr. Crowden? The Vampire? Is he the one who sent those two goons to scare me and steal my car?"

"Yeah, he probably didn't tell them to steal your car."

Well, at least I wasn't hyperventilating anymore. I pulled my knees up on the couch and wrapped my arms around them. I hadn't slept today, and the adrenaline crash was hitting me. My mind couldn't focus on anything except maybe I wasn't going to die tonight. Frankie said I probably wouldn't die. He also didn't deny that he was a mind reader. Then a thought occurred to me "Oh my God. You have been reading my mind this whole time!" I exclaimed, making him jump.

He frowned but didn't deny it.

"You should eat something, there is a place close by," Frankie said. He gave the man at the door a nod, and we walked back out into the oncoming evening. The sky was becoming a brilliant red to the west. I wasn't hungry but hadn't eaten in over twenty-four hours, so I needed to get some food into me if I was going to keep from passing out when I met this vampire guy.

"What is so special about this Mr. Crowden anyway?" I asked as we walked. The streets were empty.

"He's the oldest vampire in the city. Well, probably in the state…maybe all of the southwest. He makes and enforces the rules, so they don't go all wild and eat too many people."

"Too many? How many are too many?" I asked, getting nervous again.

"Some of them are trouble. I don't know much more about them, they keep to themselves, and we don't mingle," he said glancing back at me. "At least we didn't," he said under his breath, but I caught his words and spent a moment considering what he meant by that. We had already fallen into our usual pattern with him walking slightly ahead of me and leading the way.

"And who are you? Why do you know anything about them?"

He sighed. He had opened the door to this line of questioning. I had just stepped through it. "I am not sure you are ready to hear all that yet."

Of course, dodge the most important parts. He was probably right though, and I wasn't ready to hear more about anything weird. I was struggling enough with the vampires, and I had known about them for most of my life.

We were seated at a small diner a few blocks over. I ordered a burger and fries and a glass of soda. It was more than I could afford to spend but if I died today, I deserved to eat something that didn't come from a freezer. This was it. My last meal and I wasn't sure I'd even be able to eat it with how exhausted and terrified I was.

We sat in our usual silence, but it was no longer comfortable which made me a bit sad. I liked our silent relationship, even if he knew about me all along. You know what they say about ignorance and bliss.

The time had come. I had no choice but to get going. I trusted Frankie. I kept repeating that in my head.

I left him at the diner and took the long bus ride to the upscale neighbourhood. When I arrived, I pulled out the card in my pocket to check the address. It was full dark now, but there were street lights along the well maintained and landscaped sidewalk. The area was clean and quiet and completely free of the ranting vagrants and street thugs that littered my neighbourhood. The homes here were pretentious mansions, set well back from the road so you could only get a glimpse of the majestic buildings beyond the gates.

I found a uniformed guard sitting in a gatehouse at the address on the card. He saw me coming and raised a single brow when I hesitated. I really needed to put on my brave pants.

"Who are you?" the man asked. I should say vampire because he was not a human.

"Lark," was all I replied.

He took out a radio and spoke so softly I couldn't hear him. I couldn't hear the static reply either, but the gatekeeper looked back to me and said, "Go ahead," with a smirk.

This was really happening. I was going to walk into a house full of vampires. Why had I trusted Frankie? I could have left town. Hitchhiked or maybe stolen a bicycle. Why hadn't I thought of that? I'd had twelve hours. I should have gone. Stupid.

I entered through a smaller gate onto the lane leading to the mansion. The trees on either side were intimidating, hanging over my path. They grew denser as I went until I couldn't see beyond the driveway. I didn't care if I looked scared. I was fucking scared.

The house loomed ahead with cathedral columns supporting the second and third story balconies. The house was stone with arched windows and doorways. Very Dracula. Perfect for a house full of vampires. A total cliché. There was a five-car garage to one side, and the paved driveway branched off towards it after circling in front of the giant house.

I stood at the base of the stairs leading up to the door and paused. There was still time to turn around and leave. I could go far, far away.

Too late, the door opened, and a cheery looking older man stood in the doorway. He looked like a butler, not scary at all, but then, he was human.

Why would they have a human working for them? Was he a snack for later? I couldn't just stand there any longer; even I was getting a weird vibe from me. Ugh.

"I'm Lark," I said as I mounted the steps and approached the man.

"Yes, I was told to expect you. Come in. I'll show you to the parlour."

No turning back now, I was in the spider's web.

CHAPTER THREE

I followed the man into the foyer. It was painted in muted tones of grey and tan but had large oil paintings of sunsets and landscapes hanging on the walls. The furniture was befitting the house and matched the tone and colour pallet. The butler led me to a smaller room down a hall.

"Have a seat, Mr. Crowden shouldn't be long," he said before leaving and closing the door behind him. I didn't hear a lock click, but my nerves were on fire. I walked back over and tested the doorknob. It wasn't locked.

I stood in the middle of what looked like a lawyer's office. A large desk sat in one corner with bookshelves lining the walls behind it. The couches on the other side of the room probably had a fancy name to go with the ornate wooden scrolling on the side and back. They weren't soft and stuffed like a couch either. The ceiling in the room was over ten feet and had hammered tin sheets covering it. I walked over to the closest bookcase and pulled a random book off. It was not in English, it looked like Latin, but since I had a faulty education, at best, I had no idea.

I put the book back on the shelf and took a seat on one of the couch things. It wasn't particularly comfortable. In fact, the whole house had this 'don't get comfortable, you shouldn't be here' vibe. I would have loved to leave, but now that I was here, I was ready to see this through. As time dragged on, I got restless. The room was large enough that I could move effortlessly amongst the furniture, so I paced around.

As I passed the desk for the fourth time, I noticed some pages that looked like letters on the desk. With nothing better to do, I started reading. It seemed to be a correspondence from someone named Vaughn. Though it seemed to be in Latin too, maybe.

I glanced over a few more in the pile. They were all the same, but maybe this was my chance to learn something about these secretive vampires. I folded a couple and tucked them into my pocket then returned to the couch just as the butler walked back in.

"My, deepest apologies, Mr. Crowden won't be able to meet with you today. An emergency has come up that he must attend to, if you would follow me, I can see you to your quarters."

"I'll just head home, thanks." I slid past him into the hall.

"Mr. Crowden has asked that you remain here until he is able to meet with you. I have a suite of rooms available for you in the north tower," he said, following me out into the hall and gesturing to the north.

I looked that way and then back the other, trying to decide which direction we had come. The hall was wide and painted in earth tones, with small ornate light fixtures on the wall but looked mostly the same in both directions.

"I'm not staying here," I said with a laugh that completely lacked any humour.

"I can send someone to gather some of your belongings."

Like that was the only reason I wasn't going to stay in a house full of vampires.

"I am not staying here. You can steal all my stuff and burn down my apartment building, I'm still not staying here," I said with conviction this time. No more messing around.

The butler sighed. "Mr. Crowden thought it might be a problem for you. Please be aware that we will have a guard outside your apartment and following you until you are able to meet with Mr. Crowden properly."

"It's fine. I'll stay in town," I promised.

His face gave away nothing when he replied, "That's excellent," He turned and started walking down the hall. I hurried after him, and he led me to the front door.

He opened the door and stood to the side. I gave him a suspicious glance and walked out. I was hustling down the steps and the driveway before he could blink. I was leaving the vampire house alive and with all my blood. It seemed too good to be true. Like I had thumbed my nose at fate.

Just as I got to the guard house, a shiny Tesla pulled up outside the gates and idled. I walked to the gate, and the guard let me through. Indicating the car, he asked, "Would you like a lift home?"

"Hell no," was my reply as I peered at the vampire behind the wheel. His eyes glowed in the darkness. Apart from the freaky eyes, the guy looked like a kindergarten teacher with floppy curly hair and a soft boyish face, but I knew he was a predator waiting to pounce. All vampires were monsters, and this one was no different. I wasn't going to climb into a steel box with the devil willingly -- even if it was an expensive, eco-friendly steel box.

I immediately turned south and headed back towards the bus stop the car driving slowly behind me. I now had a vampire babysitter. Great.

I stood at the bus stop, the car idling about a hundred feet away. It was ridiculous, but I was not going to engage the vampire. He could stay in his car, and I would wait here in the dark for my bus. After waiting for half an hour, I accepted that the busses didn't run this late in this neighbourhood. I turned to start walking out of the posh area of the city and towards areas where busses would still be running to take the drunk hockey fans home from the stadium.

The car pulled up beside me, and the kindergarten-teacher-gone-vampire spoke, "I can give you a lift, it's no trouble, I'm going your way," he said flashing a toothy smile. He apparently thought he was clever.

"No, thanks," I said moving away from the car.

"Suit yourself," he replied and then stopped the car and let me walk on. Once I was about fifty feet ahead, the sound of tires rolling on the pavement told me he was following again.

As I walked, the houses got more and more dilapidated. Fewer street lights, more shadows, more people standing in shadows. Creepier.

I was looking around, trying to find the nearest bus stop when I noticed a group of men on the sidewalk, obscured by the shadow of a medium-sized apartment building. The building itself was dull and dirty, but brilliant graffiti covered the lower eight feet of the old brick exterior. The men were speaking quietly until one noticed me. They turned, and walked in my direction, taking up the entire sidewalk. They were large and hairy with full thick beards and long hair, reminding me of wild animals on the prowl.

As they approached, I glanced across the street to see if I could zip across but before I could make my escape they were in front of me. I was surrounded.

One of them wrapped his thick, steely arms around me, pinning my arms to my sides and lifting my feet off the pavement. I did what I should have done last time I was confronted with danger; I let out a deafening scream.

I thrashed about kicking at him with my heels, but I couldn't seem to make enough contact to hurt him. I flung my head back, and a curse let me know I had at least done some kind of damage, but the man didn't release me. One of the other men came up and sneered at me. I tried to kick him away, but he caught my feet and held them. Now I was suspended between the two men.

I kept screaming until a hand covered my mouth. It belonged to the man holding me. He was able to hold my upper body with just one giant arm. Damn me for being small. He wouldn't be able to do this if I were an average size person.

Suddenly one of the men let out a scream, then another. The hand covering my mouth went to my neck, squeezing. I heard a rumbled "Back off, we found her first."

There was a flash of red, and I was unceremoniously dropped to the pavement. Someone's boot swung towards my head then it was lights out, Lark.

***

There was a throbbing in the side of my head, and I couldn't open my eyes. One felt like an overripe plum ready to burst from my eye socket. I knew I was on a bed, but the lack of foul odour from the downstairs garbage bin informed me that I was not in my apartment. The sweet smell of flowers and the deafening silence confirmed it.

I peeked open my eye that still worked and took in the room. Well, half of it. Beige curtains met beige walls and carpet. It was like out of a catalogue. The furniture looked new and matched, and the ceiling was white Stucco. Everything was immaculate. I was starting to panic when I remembered being attacked.

I sat up suddenly and frantically looked around as the door opened, and Mr. Crowden's butler walked in.

The butler paused in the doorway. "Apologies, Miss Lark. I didn't mean to intrude. I thought you might be awake and came to see if you required anything."

"I want to go home," I said staggering to a standing position and stumbling towards him.

"Please if you will just wait, Mr. Crowden wants to speak with you, and you should be seen by the doctor again before you go."

I pressed past him out the door and to the top of a broad set of stairs.

"Please, wait and see the doctor at least. You have a serious injury," he said as I started down the stairs.

I turned to tell him to go to hell but got dizzy and slipped. I landed on my back and slid down a few more stairs, hitting the back of my head and jarring my arm.

I moaned and looked up to see the vampire who had followed me home standing on the stairs below me. "Why are you lying on the stairs?" he asked.

I tried to pull myself up, unsuccessfully.

"Let me help you," the vampire said reaching out towards me.

"No," I replied, flinching back from him.

"Why are you so stubborn?" he asked like I was the one being unreasonable.

"I don't know, maybe because I like my blood on the inside," I replied, and he flinched back like I had slapped him.

"You will have to excuse Randy. He is a new vampire. He is also still a bit sensitive about his status," the butler said from the top of the stairs.

I looked at Randy and looked back at the butler. You have got to be kidding me. "Are you saying he has some issues?" I asked sarcastically.

"Not all vampires wished to be vampires," he said looking sadly at Randy.

Great, now I was feeling bad for hurting a vampire's feelings. "I have to go," I said finally pulling myself up off the stairs. Randy followed me out in to the sunshine. My eyes burned, and I didn't have any sunglasses. I squinted and tried to get into the shade of the trees that lined the driveway. At the gatehouse, there was no gatekeeper, and the gate was locked.

"Hello?" I yelled, shaking the gate a bit, but then there was a buzzing sound, and the gate started rolling open. I heard tires on the pavement and glanced back to find Randy once again following behind me in his ridiculous car.

God. They didn't know when to quit. Ok so the vampire, Randy, probably saved my ass last night with those lowlifes and he hadn't drained my blood and killed me, but that didn't mean I was willing to trust a vampire.

I walked through the gate and headed for the bus stop. It was a pretty good route in the daytime. I knew I wouldn't have to wait long.

I waited. So did Randy.

My head was throbbing, and my eyes were heavy. Finally, the bus pulled up, and I boarded. Sitting in the back, I watched as Randy followed the bus, stopping at all the stops and waiting to move again.

Once home, I climbed the stairs and had a shower. Someone else in the building must have used all the hot water because I was greeted by only cold water. If felt nice on my face, but I was shivering by the time I rinsed the soap out of my hair. I heated up a microwave dinner and tried to eat some of it. My jaw ached every time I opened my mouth, but I finally managed to finish it. I washed my fork and threw away the packaging before climbing into bed. To hell with the vampire parked on the street in front of my building, his presence couldn't keep my eyes from closing or sleep from taking me under.

***

Sunday night a pounding on my door woke me, and when I glanced at my clock, it said midnight. I had never slept so late before. I missed half the night.

I rolled off my bed and tried to peel my eye open, but it was a no go. It was swollen shut and crusted over. I bet I looked super. Note to self, avoid mirrors.

"Who is it?" I asked as I stumbled towards the door.

"It's me," Frankie said from the other side.

I swung the door open and turned to make coffee. Frankie had never been in my apartment, but since he knew all the secrets in my head, there was no point in keeping him out of my room. I pointedly kept all my thoughts to making coffee.

I heard the door close behind him but kept busy for a few more minutes. I could feel his eyes drilling into the back of my head. When I finally faced him, his blank face immediately flashed to rage.

"Who did this?" he asked stepping closer to me.

"Some assholes on the street. I was walking home from the vampire's house, and they jumped me."

"Why were you walking home? You should have taken the bus!" he sounded vicious with a slight growl to his voice. I took a step back. He noticed and took two deep breaths then blanked his face. "Answer me, why didn't you take the bus?"

"Because, nosey parker, the busses had stopped running by the time I left."

"Why didn't they drive you home?" he asked shortly with his anger rising again.

"Calm down, God, they offered, but I didn't want to ride with a vampire," I said, grabbing a bag of peas from the freezer and holding it to my face. It was probably too late for that, but I hoped it would help a little.

A little louder and not calmer at all, he replied: "Then you should have called me!"

"You don't have a car!" I shot back exasperated with this whole conversation.

He shook his head and ignored my argument completely, "Where were these people that jumped you?" he was growling again.

"Out by the hockey stadium, maybe two blocks north of it," I said, pointing uselessly at the wall.

With that information, he turned on his heel and stormed out, slamming my door behind him. Thankfully my front door was sturdier than my face.

CHAPTER FOUR

I spent the rest of the night in my apartment. My advanced yoga class was in the morning, and I wasn't willing to give up on my dream just because a bunch of Neanderthals jumped me. I would have to ice my face and hope it looked at least somewhat better by 7 AM.

It didn't.

Everyone stared as I entered the gym. The muscular man behind the counter looked at me, pity flashing across his face. He handed me a flyer for women's self-defence class. Not a bad idea, actually. It was on Tuesday mornings immediately after my yoga class. I would be exhausted from work and then yoga, but I could probably manage it.

I signed up and then continued to the locker rooms.

Yoga was brutal, all my sore muscles shook with exertion, and I found new things that hurt. The pain started in my leg halfway through class, and the throbbing only served to remind me that I would still have to walk back to the bus stop with my gym bag. That was going to suck. Our instructor, or Yogi, Shanti, tried to help me, but I was all over the place.

Near the end of class, I glanced over and saw Randy sitting by the front door of the gym, reading a magazine about bodybuilding. When I hadn't seen him outside my apartment in the morning, I thought he must have gone off to do vampire things. Things I didn't want to know about.

Shanti led us through some meditation. Sitting in our rows on the floor, I let my mind drift and shut out the pain I felt.

"Lark."

I opened my eyes to Shanti's smiling face.

"You must have gone into deep meditation, I was going to leave you till you came back naturally, but the next class is coming in."

I looked up at the clock and realized I had lost nearly half an hour. I should have felt calmer, but as I stood up the pain in my leg throbbed and I angry instead.

The pain must have made me a little stupid. It's the only excuse for what happened next. I marched up to Randy and demanded "I want my car back," putting my hands on my hips like an angry school teacher.

His reply was cool and composed. "You will have to talk to Mr. Crowden about your car. I can take you back to the estate now if you wish."

I didn't bother answering him. I just narrowed my eyes and turned back to the locker rooms. As long as I was still alive, I had work to do and rent to pay.

Of course, he followed the bus in his car. What kind of vampire drove a freaking Tesla anyway?

After a fitful sleep, I had a shower, got dressed and left for work. I needed extra travel time since my poor car was being held, hostage. The longer I was without it, the more I treasured its memory. It wasn't a great car, but it had never let me down.

"Lark, can I speak to you for a minute?" Mr. Fellum called, as I walked in to work that evening.

I stepped into his office without a word. His eyes raked over my bruised and swollen features, and I tensed at his scrutiny.

"What happened, Lark?"

"I fell down." I had fallen, it wasn't really a lie I just had some help in the falling part.

He watched me in silence for a moment before he spoke again. "You should be more careful."

"I will." Moving to leave, he didn't stop me, so I put my stuff in the break room and went on shift. It would be a long night, but at least I was still alive.

Monday nights were always quiet. I had the usual moms grabbing a few items, kids getting candy, some drunks, but it was mainly quiet. I spent some time thinking about all the ways my life could get worse.

I could see Randy's car in the parking lot the whole night. I wasn't sure how he slept. Maybe vampires didn't need to sleep. Put that on the list of things I might know about vampires.

About 3 AM, the bell above the bell above the door chimed. A man walked to the back of the store and picked out some items from the refrigerator section.

As he turned back towards the cash, I caught his pale face and realized he was the vamp from the bar the other night.

"Good evening," he said in his refined voice while setting yogurt and juice on the counter. Apparently, he didn't recognize me. Thank God.

"Find everything you were looking for?" I asked. Did vamps eat yogurt?

He paused for a second looking at me. "Not hardly," he said before dropping a twenty on the counter.

I wasn't going to fall into his trap. I took the money and handed him back his change.

"Thank you, Amelia," he said.

He was out the door before I picked up my chin off the ground. I had gone by Lark my whole adult life. I wasn't Amelia anymore. That name belonged to a happy girl who lived a different life. A life without vampires.

The fact that a vampire knew the name sent a cold sweat down my back. Did every vampire know who I was and what I could do? The walls were closing in on me.

I couldn't even go hide in my hovel. My shift wasn't over for a few more hours. I looked out the door, and Randy's car was gone. Shit. When had he left? Why had he left?

I spent the next few hours jumping every time the door chimed, but I made it to the end of my shift. The sun was just peeking up between the buildings, but it didn't comfort me like it usually did. I hopped on the bus and made it home in one piece, but I still had to go to yoga and self-defence. I wanted to hide away but knew I wasn't safe at home either.

Hopefully, the class would help me relax. I was ok. That's all I needed to keep repeating to myself. I was alive. Of course, I missed the bus I needed to get to yoga class on time and showed up just as it was starting, disturbing Shanti, and everyone in the class.

It was an excellent class, but I couldn't focus. My breathing never settled, and my concentration was zero.

Self-defence was a different story.

"Welcome to women's self-defence," the instructor said. "My name is Laurie. In this class, you will be learning defence and evasion techniques. Don't worry if you aren't strong, these skills don't require you to be stronger than your attacker, just smarter, and I guarantee you are smarter than anyone who tries to mess with you after you have taken this class."

That sounded hopeful. I couldn't wait to get started. The instructor paired us off and demonstrated proper technique for evading and escaping. We began with wrist grabs and moved up to choke holds. The end of class was about kicking and punching. She had us line up in front of punching bags and practice punching and kicking technique. I hadn't expected the adrenaline rush I got from the class.

"Next class we will have our live dummy to help you work on your techniques with full force. It is a man, dressed in heavy padding. If some of you can't handle that yet" --she looked at me-- "because you have been victimized and aren't ready to relive that trauma with a live attacker, I will have the punching bags set up to practice on as well. Please don't feel pressured to participate if you aren't comfortable."

Apparently, everyone thought I was in an abusive relationship. Whatever, I had no interest in sharing with the class. I thanked her and left. I already felt more in control and capable. A class of punching and kicking helped much more than yoga. Why didn't I discover this sooner?

I hit the locker room for a quick shower. Unlike my apartment, the water here was always hot, and the shower stall was bigger than a school locker. I got dressed in black jeans and t-shirt and tied my wet hair up in a ponytail.

When I walked out of the gym a half hour later, I slid my sunglasses on momentarily before abruptly taking them off again when I noticed my old Honda was parked right in front, engine running. There was no one in sight, but there must have been a vampire somewhere nearby. Something seemed different, but I couldn't put my finger on it until I got in and shut the door. The car was quiet. The muffler which had been rattling so loud it would vibrate the whole vehicle, particularly when in reverse, was silent.

Weird.

I turned the radio on, and the dial didn't stick, it turned smoothly. The blown-out passenger side speaker had lost the muffled, gritty sound.

The ride home was smooth, the potholes on the old roads were no longer teeth rattling. I got home and parked, got out of the car and took a walk around. New tires, I hadn't noticed.

When I released the trunk, it opened. It hadn't opened when I bought the car, so I never used the trunk. Ok, so the vampires did some things to my car while they had it. Maybe one of them was a mechanic.

Still, it didn't sit well with me. I wasn't a charity and fixing my car didn't change what kind of monsters they were. I locked the car and went back to my apartment. The sun was getting high in the sky, and I was exhausted.

When I woke that night, I was restless. I didn't want to sit at home alone all night so sent a text to Frankie: want to go out?

He replied a moment later: meet you downstairs in 20

Perfect. I got dressed quickly and zipped out the door.

Frankie was waiting at the bottom of the stairs. When he saw me, he turned on his heel and started walking down the road. Not towards Arnie's though, he was headed towards the warehouse he had taken me to the day the vampires had summoned me. He did his fancy knock and the guy who had let us in the first time swung open the door. Frankie walked inside and disappeared into the darkness. My eyes took an extra second to adjust, but I could make out his shape across the open space.

"What are you?" I asked, and that was the right question. I had hoped to be a little bit drunk for this conversation though.

He snorted a laugh and opened a bottle, taking a sip before handing it to me.

"Thanks," the mind reading thing was maybe not so bad. I mean, it's possible I had thought some random dirty thoughts while we drank in the past, but as long as he wasn't spreading gossip about me, we were probably cool.

His white teeth glinted in the low light, and I knew he had been listening.

I thought every swear word I knew at him, including some super dirty ones, until he laughed out loud.

When he got control of himself, he looked at me and lost all the humour. "I'm a warlock," he said straight-faced.

I laughed this time. "Magic and shit?" I had honestly assumed everything else was probably true as well. If vampires are real, why not magic and fairies and whatnot.

He looked conflicted like he didn't really want to tell me the answer but when he did speak again, all he said was "Sort of," which cleared up absolutely nothing.

I snorted. "What is this place then? Some kind of warlock secret meeting place?"

"You could call it that. It's a place of power in the city. A safe place. But it is kind of a secret."

"You know all my secrets," I complained.

"It's not safe for you to know any more right now. You'll have to trust me a bit longer."

That was the moment I realized he knew that I trusted him. He had plucked the thought out of my head the last time we were here and could easily take advantage of that trust since I had no idea if it was misplaced or not. Gah, things were easier when I didn't know any of this when we were just two people sitting on bar stools.

"We were never just two people, Lark. But let's go to Arnie's. We can pretend it's like it used to be."

"Ok," I said and followed him back out the door. The night had truly fallen now, and the darkness in the alley was sharp in contrast to the light of the street lamp which cut across the entrance.

The streets were quiet tonight. Tuesday night was not a big party night for anyone. As we turned the corner to get to the bar, we came upon a group of men but as soon as they spotted us, they dispersed quietly. Once we were passed, I looked over to Frankie whose face betrayed nothing. Now that I thought about it, no one had ever bothered me when I walked with Frankie. He was tall but not particularly rough looking. He was clean-shaven, and if it weren't for his leather jacket, he would look almost bookish.

Frankie looked at me, and I knew that he had read my thoughts, but he seemed disinclined to fill in the details for me, so I let it go too. I just wanted a bit of normal like he had offered and talking about the thugs would probably not be normal. I'd just have to remember to walk the streets with Frankie at night – never alone.

"You can walk the streets safely. I have made sure everyone knows not to bother you," he said, apparently not hiding the fact he was reading my mind anymore.

"You can't control the drug dealers and muggers," I said, sure he was exaggerating.

He winked at me, "Can't I?"

That conversation was threatening to get really not-normal really fast. If he had some kind of power over the evil of our neighbourhood, I didn't want to hear about it tonight.

Arnie's was quiet, as I predicted. A couple older guys watching the sports on the TV and sipping beers and then there was us. We sat at the bar, in our usual seats. Gin and tonic, rum and coke, empty seat between us. Arnie turned on the music, and I let my mind chill. I tried not to think about vampires or magic, but that was impossible. I started to wonder what else Frankie could do. Maybe he could fix me, so I didn't see vampires anymore. Would I be safe then? Argh, I was ruining it.

Frankie slid onto the seat between us, and his elbow brushed against mine on the bar and said: "You are fine just as you are."

I sighed.

"You don't understand. Move back one seat. God." I shooed him away from me.

He laughed and shifted back over. We drank quietly for a while before the bar started to get busy. Some people were playing pool in the back, a group of girls were at the bar drinking fruity drinks and giggling about something. Probably boys. I had never bothered trying to make friends. I moved too often after my family was gone.

Frustrated, I kicked my booted feet under my bar stool, time for another drink. I waved to Arnie, and he smiled and slid a drink to me. "Thanks, Arnie," I waved.

A man wearing a leather jacket like Frankie's sat down at the bar and started talking to him about something quietly. I had never seen anyone else in that jacket, so I watched them out of the corner of my eye for a few minutes, but I was getting stir crazy and decided to go check out the pool tables. I knew how to play but wasn't very good. Usually, I shot balls around, trying to organize the balls on the table by colour. It was like a Zen garden except I got to smash the rocks with a pointy stick.

After about twenty minutes or so, the guys playing pool at the other table went back to the bar leaving me alone in the back room. Arnie came in every now and then to take my empty glass and leave me a full one, but otherwise, it was empty. The voices and music from the main bar were muted back here, leaving me to my thoughts.

If I moved to the left side of the table, I could see the back of Frankie's head. I thought at him that his ears were elfish, and he put a hand up to feel his ear. Ha. That was a fun trick. I turned back around and lined up a shot. That was when I felt eyes on me. I glanced under my arm and saw the vampire who had been here last time and bought yogurt at the Discount Emporium. He was just leaning against the wall in the shadow of the far corner, by the vacant pool table – watching me.

Weirdo.

I ignored him as long as I could before turning and glaring. "What do you want?"

He didn't speak immediately, so I set the pool cue down and grabbed my drink. I walked back to where Frankie was still chatting with the same guy. My seat was occupied, but I was ready to go anyway. I downed my drink and set the glass on the bar. Frankie said goodbye to the guy and walked towards the door. I followed behind him and out into the cold night air

"There was a vampire, and he has been following me, I think," I said. Frankie hadn't asked and probably already knew. If he did know, he didn't seem concerned.

"I can't interfere. I said I wouldn't as long as you weren't in danger," he said mysteriously.

Argh. "What does that even mean? I don't understand you! Can't you just give me a straight answer?"

"I told him I would let it be. You should talk to him," he replied, making zero sense.

"Talk to the vampire?" I shouted incredulously. We had stopped in the middle of the empty sidewalk. Deep shadows were hiding the storefronts and the alley, but we were directly under a street light. From where I stood, I couldn't see Frankie's face because he was backlit by the lamp.

Things were so messed up.

A limo pulled up beside us, and I recognized Randy behind the wheel. He had been absent for a few days, but I felt like I was being watched occasionally. He lowered the passenger window and leaned across the center console to look at me. "Mr. Crowden would like to speak with you if you can spare a moment."

I looked at Frankie, but he avoided my gaze. Fine. That was how it was.

"Sure, Randy, let's do this," I said throwing my hands in the air. Maybe it was the alcohol that caused my poor decision, but if Frankie wouldn't fill me in, maybe this vamp would tell me what was up before he ate me.

"He won't eat you," Frankie muttered unhappily. The mind reading thing was already getting old, and I narrowed my eyes at Frankie to make sure he knew I was done with that. Randy hopped out and zipped around the front of the car, ushering me towards the back. He opened the door, and when I slid inside, he closed it again. Before I could blink, we were moving down the road.

The limo went around the block and stopped in front of Arnie's. I opened my mouth to ask Randy what he was doing when the door opened, and that weird vamp that had been watching me slipped inside. He shut the door and then we were moving again.

"Hello, Amelia," he said in that suave tone he seemed partial to. I cringed at his use of my old name.

"So, you are Mr. Crowden then?" When he nodded, I continued, "Call me Lark,"

"I'm not calling you that."

"It's my name," I said shortly.

"No, it isn't. Your name is Amelia Rose Clark. That is the name your parents gave you."

Insta-panic.   He   knew   too   much.

CHAPTER FIVE

"Stop the car," I said loud enough for Randy to hear me. He looked back at Mr. Crowden in the rear-view mirror. "I said stop the car," I nearly yelled, panic escalating in my voice as I pulled on the door handle.

The limo pulled over, and I pushed the door hard to get out before slamming it behind me and striding off down the road. We were only half a dozen blocks from my apartment, close enough to walk.

A vampire talking about my family was as close to a death threat as I could think of. There was a reason I changed my name and moved to a different state. This was a new life. One that I had made for myself. I didn't care that I lived in a shitty apartment or drove a shitty car when those things were mine. This life was mine. It didn't belong to vampires. Vampires ruined everything. If Mr. Crowden wanted to kill me, fine, but I wasn't going to be the mouse he toyed with.

I walked along the dirty, darkened streets - followed by a sleek and shiny limousine. The night was chilly, but my blood still ran hot, and my mind was spinning.

How did he even know who I was? Was he involved somehow in what had happened to my family, or did he hack some database to get my history? Ugh.

I was in the dark all the time, while my whole life story was, apparently, an open book. Something had to change.

I remembered the letters I had taken from the vampire house. Google could help translate them. Maybe they held useful information.

It was nearly daybreak by the time I was home. Crawling into bed would have been perfect, but I had an early class, so I threw on my yoga clothes and headed back down to my car. It was still parked where I had left it. Thank God!

Wednesday morning was my senior's yoga class. I took a deep breath and let go of the anger and fear and guilt brought up by the vampire because I loved this class. The little old ladies giggled like school girls as they did modified yoga poses, and the dirty old men waggled their eyebrows at the ladies. I couldn't help loving them all. Seeing them made me think of my parents and what they would be like now if they had survived. It also made me wonder if I would grow old with someone too, someday, and if we would take some class together at the gym.

When the last pair of grey-haired sweethearts had walked out, I went to the aerobics room and booked a treadmill. Running was my least favourite exercise, but it was, hands down, the best workout bang for your buck, so I forced myself to do it twice a week.

I was jamming out to the heavy metal music that came with the iPod I bought at the pawn shop last payday and getting my heart rate up when the ass, Mr. Crowden, walked in wearing sweats and took up the treadmill beside me.

"What are you doing?" I asked, pulling out an earbud.

"Hmm? Oh, just getting in a workout," he replied casually. Great.

"You don't even go to this gym." Do vampires even need to work out?

"I do now. I needed a new gym; mine was quite boring." He turned the speed up to full, and the sound of the machine cut off our conversation – such as it was.

Bitter at having to share my gym with him, I put my earbud back in and turned the volume up a bit more. I focused on the far wall and just ran. I definitely ran harder and longer than usual. My legs were threatening to give out, so I hit the stop button and moved to the walking track that circled the room to cool down.

Of course, he walked up beside me. Between the metal music and my anger at his invasion of my sacred space, I got a bit bolder than I should have.

"Why haven't you killed me?" I asked the vampire. A man with a ponytail on an elliptical looked at me. Hmm, maybe I should whisper.

Mr. Crowden chuckled. Apparently, he wasn't winded at all from his run. "I have no interest in killing you while I have a need for your skills."

I stopped dead, and he kept walking. "What do you mean?" I asked louder as he was still moving away from me.

"As I said, you have a skill. I require that skill for a project."

"Why would I do anything for you?" I asked hotly, walking after him but his long legs still carried him farther. Being short was dumb.

Suddenly he was in front of me. His eyes were burning into mine from inches away. "Pretty brave. I can think of one excellent reason why you would do as I ask, but I don't think I need to spell it out for you."

Shit. Holy shit!

I turned on my heel and hurried back to the locker room, but when I chanced a look behind me, he was gone. I should get in my car and leave. Now that he knew about me, it was always going to be like this; like walking on the edge of a knife. It would be better off in a city where no one knew about me. No matter what Frankie said, I couldn't just trust that he wouldn't eventually kill me even if he had a use for me right now.

Back in my street clothes, I walked out of the building and immediately dropped my gym bag as anger crashed over me. My car was gone. Again. That rat bastard! I spun in a circle looking for any vampire. Not one was in sight. I was so done with this. I called a cab and sat on the curb. I didn't have money to be throwing away on cabs, but I was exhausted and just wanted to go home.

A car pulled up in front of me, and the window lowered. It wasn't a cab.

"You want a lift?" Randy asked from the driver's seat of his Tesla.

"I already called a cab, move along, vamp," I replied, still completely annoyed.

"I don't think that cab will be coming. I'll drive you home though."

If the bastard had cancelled my cab, I would have to take the bus with my gym bag. "Frig. Why can't you people leave me alone?" I asked, exasperated.

"Get in, please?" He asked. He looked so innocent and not at all like a monster.

I considered my options then opened the door and jammed myself and my gym bag in the passenger seat.

"Can you take me to my car?" I asked hopefully.

"Sorry, the boss doesn't want you running away. I can drive you anywhere you want to go." He put the car in drive and drove towards my apartment.

Randy seemed like he was maybe an ok guy, for a vampire. Perhaps he would be on my side. "Why is he doing this?"

Randy just kept driving for a while, chewing his lip like he wanted to say something. So, I let him consider his words. After a while he whispered, softly "he is the boss, he doesn't usually have to ask nicely to get what he wants, but you have powerful protection."

"What protection?" I asked.

He just bit his lip and shook his head.

"Please? I have no idea what to do or who to trust," I said hoping the truth might convince him to spill it.

"Look, don't tell anyone I told you, ok? But your friend is a freaking powerful warlock and can basically do what he wants. There is a treaty that won't allow him to act first, but his wrath would be … uhm, unpleasant."

I snorted. "Frankie? Huh. Well, that's good for me." I trailed off. Thinking about all the things Frankie had said about me being safe and that I won't be bothered by anyone anymore. Maybe there was truth to his words. I assumed his promises were more for my peace of mind than an actual guarantee.

I pulled out my phone and sent a text to Frankie: Are you a complete badass?

I got his reply a moment later: pretty much.

Huh, well there you go. Even if I had no idea what the hell I was stepping into, having someone who demanded respect at my back, was probably an excellent start.

Since I had Randy here and he seemed in a sharing mood, it was time to start Vampires 101.

"Tell me about this treaty, Randy."

"Uhm, I shouldn't have said anything. I'll get in trouble if he finds out."

"Mr. Crowden?"

He nodded but seemed nervous, so I let it go.

"Do vampires eat food?" I asked, hoping that line of questioning wouldn't get anyone in trouble.

"Oh yes, we eat just like humans do," he said relaxing now that we had stepped away from the touchy subject. "We are just like humans except we don't sleep and drink blood." He seemed to realize his words and frowned. I didn't want to hear about them drinking blood.

At least it answered the yogurt question. I would have to find a different way to find out about this treaty, starting with translating those borrowed letters.

When I got home, I booted up my laptop and started typing in words from the first letter. It all seemed very ordinary and boring. It talked about a trip this Vaughn person had taken and something about taking care of a family. Nothing incriminating at all but google translate did a pretty poor job of making sense of them.

That evening I took Randy's offer of a drive to work and made it through my shift without a vampire in the store. Thursday morning, I struggled through my advanced yoga class, and that night I was back at the store and stacking soup cans on a shelf when a throat cleared behind me. I knew it was Mr. Crowden. I had no thoughts that he might have decided to leave me alone, but I was so tired of this game and just wanted it over with.

"What do you want?" I asked him, not turning around.

"I would like to speak to you about a job opportunity," he said tightly. Like it was literally hurting him to be civilized at this point.

"What?" I asked, turning towards him.

"I'm asking for your help," he said shortly before taking a deep calming breath. I swear he counted to ten in his head before he continued. "I would appreciate a few moments of your time, at a place and time convenient to you. Please let Randy know."

He turned to leave, and as he got to the door, I called out "I want my car back." He didn't stop and was out the door without replying. Jerk.

In the wee hours of Friday morning, as I was getting ready to leave, my boss called me into his office for our weekly visit. The bruising on my face was now easily covered with makeup, so I looked presentable. I grabbed my stuff from the break room, and Mr. Fellum ushered me into his office. My shift was the same as last week, but I had the Sunday night shift too. So, I only had two nights off. I should pick an evening to meet with the vampire. He was not going to leave me alone, apparently, and maybe what he wanted wasn't so terrible. A job offer didn't sound bad. Unless it involved selling my blood to him. Ugh. Only one way to find out.

I walked up to the Tesla as the doors unlocked, climbed in and turned to Randy. "I can meet him tonight at Arnie's around nine."

Randy's face lit up like a Christmas tree. "You won't regret it, Mr. Crowden is a good man. I promise."

I scoffed at Randy's enthusiasm. Super vamp hadn't killed me yet, so that gave me hope but I wasn't ready to trust a vampire. I couldn't imagine why he would have a job for me either. I didn't exactly have a stellar education or resume.

Randy pulled away from the curb. I was lost in thought when he pulled over and stopped the car. I snapped back to the present. We were outside my apartment, so I hopped out and mumbled my thanks. He pulled up to the parking space and shut off the engine. I guess agreeing to meet Mr. Crowden wasn't enough to get Randy out of babysitting duty.

That evening I sent a text to Frankie to invite him to Arnie's too. The more, the merrier, right? Now that I knew he was some kind of super badass, I wanted him to back me up.

He agreed, but I didn't tell him I was meeting Mr. Fang-face. Better to beg forgiveness than ask permission.

The bang on my door let me know Frankie was ready to go, so I grabbed my keys and hustled out, trailing after him. It was ten to nine when we rounded the corner and Arnie's came in sight. A limo was parked outside. Fancy cars did not typically come to this neighbourhood, much less stop for a drink at Arnie's, so I guess my vamp had arrived.

"Were you expecting him?" Frankie muttered.

"I said I would meet him here."

Frankie snorted, "Am I your bodyguard tonight?"

He didn't sound unhappy, and when he looked at me with a slight smirk on his face, I just smiled back and shrugged one shoulder.

He didn't say anymore as we walked on. He held the door, and I stepped into a packed bar. It might have been a Friday night, but I had never seen so many people at Arnie's. Scratch that, these were vampires.

"Seems a bit rude, actually," I muttered, "he doesn't need this many vampires here."

Frankie cleared his throat and whispered, "Actually, if he offends me, he would need this many vamps here if he hoped to walk away."

I gave him the universal 'holy crap' face as we were ushered to the back room with the pool tables by Mr. Cowden's butler. That guy got around, apparently.

"Thank you for agreeing to meet me," Mr. Crowden said tightly.

I smiled at his obvious discomfort. "No problem, what can I do for you?" Ok, I might have been a bit cocky with my super-wizard standing beside me.

The vampire's eyes glowed brightly for a second and then simmered down. "I have a proposal for you. You see, vampires can't identify other vampires by sight. Unless we are familiar with each other, of course. This poses a problem when trying to identify rogue trouble-makers, as you can imagine. I would require your services to track and identify these corrupt vampires. In exchange, I will pay you a decent salary and supply you with accommodation and transportation.

I scoffed, "You want me to wander around looking for vampires? Are you crazy? I'll be toast the first night. No."

I swear he was counting to ten again. "I will supply protection," he paused smugly, "Obviously."

"Oh," I stammered, "Well, that makes a difference." Wait, was I considering this? I shook my head "This is ridiculous, I can't go looking for that kind of trouble, and you can't guarantee my safety."

"You should think about it," Frankie whispered beside me.

I turned on him. "Are you in on this get Lark dead plan? I thought you were on my side, or at least not on team vampire."

Arnie walked in then and handed me a drink. I noticed nobody seemed to care that Arnie was hearing some things that might make normal people question. I tucked that piece of information away to ponder later and downed my drink.

When I set my empty glass down on the side of the pool table, Frankie replied, "Lark, this is a serious problem that affects many people. Human people. You must have noticed the problem our city has with missing people."

Of course, I had noticed. I knew better than anyone what happened when vampires got their hands-on people. Argh. Why couldn't they just handle their own problems?

"I already have a job," I said. Obviously, I couldn't do this vampire hunting business.

Mr. Crowden scoffed, "Yes. I have seen your job. I'm sure a human could do that."

"I'm a human."

He flashed his fangs at me, "You can't possibly be that stupid."

"Fuck you" I turned to leave, but a bunch of vamps blocked my way. Frankie stepped between me and the vamps.

Mr. Crowden muttered "For crying out loud" under his breath. I heard him, though I think he meant for me to hear him. Then louder he said, "I'm sorry, please don't leave."

I spun back to glare at him. Frankie moved back to the Vampire and whispered something to him. I narrowed my eyes at the traitor warlock but when he turned back, the vampires blocking our exit scattered and we left peacefully out the front door of Arnie's. I trailed along, unsure what had just happened, playing it over in my head to try and make the pieces of information fit. Did that vampire just imply I wasn't human and what the heck is Arnie?

"What did you say to him?" I asked.

"I just suggested he get his head out of his ass," Frankie chuckled "That vampire has been king of the hill for too long, maybe."

I had no frame of reference for vampire behaviour except for the slaughter of my parents. Everyone seemed to think there were 'not so bad' vampires and 'really bad' vampires. I had to think on this some more.

Thankfully when we got back to the building, Frankie started climbing the stairs to my apartment. I had some questions for him that were long past due and cornering him in my apartment was probably the best way to get my answers. All those questions flew from my head as we rounded the last corner and my smashed open door came into view.

Frankie took the last few steps a couple at a time and made it through the door while I was still trying to wrap my head around the fact my apartment had been broken in to.

I climbed the stairs more cautiously and stepped over what remained of my front door. The place was a disaster. My cruddy couch was sliced open and overturned, clothes from my bedroom were spread on the floor, every dish was broken, and knives were stuck in my table, standing on end like terrifying soldiers. This wasn't a burglary; this was a message.

CHAPTER SIX

Frankie emerged from my small bedroom, cell phone to his ear, speaking so quietly, if I hadn't seen his lips moving, I would have thought he wasn't speaking at all. He quickly pocketed his phone and started grabbing my clothes off the floor.

"Whoa, what are you doing?" I asked, snatching my undies out of his hand and then gathering some more of my more delicate items before he could.

"You can't stay here. It's time to go."

"What do you mean? Who did this? Where would I even go?" I grabbed a backpack that had somehow survived the explosion from the hook by the door and started stuffing things inside. My laptop had been hidden under some towels in the closet, where I always hide it in case anyone ever broke in and the letters I had taken from Mr. Crowden were tucked inside, so I jammed it in my bag. I was having trouble getting a good panic going, probably because I had been in panic mode for most of the last week. I just copied Frankie's movements until I had a bunch of clothes bagged up.

"Let's go," was all he said before he stepped over the broken front door and down the stairs. Just as he disappeared, my body kicked back into gear, and I hurried to catch up to him. Being alone in my trashed apartment-turned-death-threat didn't seem like a great idea.

"Where are we even going?" I called. He was at the bottom of the stairs now, walking out of view. When I cleared the bottom step, Randy's Tesla was parked on the street. Frankie was holding the door open and had tossed his armload of my clothes into the back seat.

I stopped dead and looked between Randy's face in the driver's seat and Frankie's holding the door open. The message was clear. "I don't want to go back to the vampire house."

"I have to go find these people and take care of them. You have to be safe while I'm doing that."

"I'll be safe with you, though."

Frankie sighed, "Not where I'm going."

We stood in a silent standoff for a few long moments before I finally relented and got in the car.

As the car pulled away from the curb, Frankie disappeared. One moment he was standing on the sidewalk, the next he was gone. I pressed my face against the window to try and see behind us, but he was gone. Apparently, I needed Warlock 101 too.

I didn't speak on the drive back to Mr. Crowden's house, but that didn't stop Randy from filling me in on the house itself, the staff and the other vampires who lived there. He lived in the house too, and though he had grown on me, I hadn't met any other vampires and wasn't sure how much safer

I would be there, not to mention, Mr. Crowden was a bit of an ass. Staying in his house was probably not going to be pleasant.

The sun was just peeking over the horizon at the end of the street as we turned into the driveway. I had my Saturday morning yoga class in an hour, but I called up the gym and informed them I wouldn't make it because my apartment had been broken in to. Best to keep as much truth in your lies as possible and my apartment HAD been broken in to. I was crashing and could barely keep my eyes open as Randy pulled up to the front doors of the mansion.

The butler was holding the door as I gathered my loose clothes and full backpack. Then climbed out and mounted the steps.

"Good evening, Miss. Lark," he said as I walked through the door. I just nodded and gave him a tight smile.

Randy grabbed the extra stuff I awkwardly carried and led the way through the immense mansion to an intricately carved door. He hitched my clothes under one arm and swung the door open. This was not the room I had woken up in after my run-in with the thugs on the street. Inside was a much nicer room than I had ever been in. The walls were covered by an ornate crushed velvet wallpaper in shades of burgundy and silver which was accented by the hammered chrome bed frame and burgundy window coverings. The bed was dressed in black silk sheets, and the floor was a high gloss dark mahogany. I could easily picture the room in one of the home designer magazines I sometimes skimmed through at the store.

Randy dropped my stuff on the bed and turned to me. "This is your room. The kitchen is on the main floor, and it's fully stocked, but if there is something you need, just let Drake know. You have your own bathroom." Across the room, he opened the door to what appeared to be a luxurious bathroom.

"Who is Drake?" I asked, dropping my bag on the bed.

"He is the house manager. He said hi to you at the door."

"Oh, I thought he was a butler." I walked over to check out the bathroom. It was as fancy as I expected. Beautiful granite counters, a claw foot soaker tub and marble shower stall. It looked like it was stocked with soaps and shampoos too, thankfully.

"I guess it's the same thing, but butler is such an outdated word. House manager sounds cooler."

I chuckled, "I guess that's true. Thanks, Randy," he smiled with his lips closed. I noticed he had started doing that around me like he didn't want me to see his fangs. I couldn't help but feel for him. He was kind of soft and gentle, not even close to my idea of a monster.

Randy waved, walked out the door and closed it behind him. I flicked the lock, went back into the bathroom, and turned on the bathtub taps. My apartment only had a shower, so I hadn't had a bath in a long time. I added some soap I found on the side of the tub and waited for it to fill. The water was scalding, and every time I checked, it was still really hot. I ended up adding some cold water before I could get in. I was still nervous but with the bedroom door locked and the bathroom door locked I felt almost safe enough to relax for a few minutes. I dunked under the water in the giant tub. It was probably big enough to be a hot tub. I soaked for a while but kept dozing off so got out and changed into some pyjamas before crawling under the soft, smooth sheets and falling asleep.

"Good Evening, Lark," a deep, cultured voice intoned, pulling me from my sleep.

My eyes sprung open, and I sat up so fast the room spun. It took me a second to remember where I was, but then I was in full flight mode. I swung off the far side of the bed and backed away from the voice and the vampire it belonged to.

"What are you doing in my room?" I asked indignantly.

He sat, legs crossed, in an armchair in the corner, looking like a loose imitation of a refined gentleman. If it hadn't been for his glowing eyes, I would have believed the farce. "This is actually my room since it is in my house, but I would like to speak with you about your job."

"God, have you never heard of knocking? Go away. I have to get dressed."

"Very well. I'll meet you in the study." He stood and left, closing the open door behind him.

I crossed the room and relocked the door. Apparently, that wouldn't stop super vamp from coming in, but it was all I had. In the bathroom, I caught a glimpse of my hair in the mirror. My usually low maintenance hair had turned against me. It was sticking up in places and twisted around like wind knots in a wild mustang's mane. Super. I hopped in the shower quickly and tamed the crazy with extra conditioner then got dressed and wandered out to find the study.

I passed a large dining hall with about a dozen people, scratch that, Vampires sitting around a large table eating and chatting quietly. Flashing eyes and ragged teeth. A few of them looked up as I passed the open doorway in search of the elusive study. My apartment had one benefit, you couldn't get lost in it. This mansion was basically a maze with several different levels.

I finally bumped into Drake, the house manager, and he led me to the study.

Mr. Crowden faced away from the door, leaning back in his desk chair on an apparently silent phone call with someone. When he spun around, I saw his lips moving silently like Frankie's had last night. It must have been some kind of super thing. Super vamp, super warlock. Whatever.

Mr. Super vamp ended his call and set his cell on the desk. "You look a little better." He smiled. Prick.

"What do you expect; coming into my room uninvited?"

"I won't remind you that it's my room since we have things to discuss and no time for inconsequential semantics." He stood and strolled around to the front of his desk, then leaned against it, facing me. I was still standing just inside the doorway, but he motioned me to take a seat in front of him.

Instead, I just narrowed my eyes and remained a safe distance from the bloodsucker. He grinned and continued.

"I would like you to start right away. Tonight, if possible."

I snorted "I thought we discussed this and decided it was too dangerous and stupid."

He sighed and rubbed the back of his neck, "I will keep you protected. You won't be in any danger."

I decided to switch tactics, "I already have a job. Two actually, I teach yoga twice a week."

He hummed for a moment then continued "You can continue to teach yoga, it's your night job that has to go. I'm sure it won't take them long to replace you.

"You can't actually tell me what to do. It's my life."

"It's only your life because I allow you to keep living it."

I spun on my heel intent on escaping, but he was there a second later, blocking my exit. "You can't just keep running away. You are the only person who can fill this position, and you will do this."

His eyes were glowing like the headlights of a car, and I was caught. Nowhere to go, my heart pounding in my chest like a steel drum. "Just kill me and get it over with. I've been waiting for another one of you demons to find me for most of my life. It's not like I can stop you."

He scoffed, "This is a pointless conversation. I'm not going to kill you."

"Argh, then why are you always threatening me? Get out of my way." I tried to push him, but he was made of stone, apparently.

"I have tried to ask nicely, but you don't seem to respond to that either, so, tell me, how do I get you to do this? What will it take?"

"This a negotiation now?" I mumbled, stepping back from the monster turned businessman.

"Yes, what do you want? You must want something."

Of course, I knew what I wanted. What I had been working towards for years but there was no way this vamp would ever give it to me. "I want my own yoga studio."

"Done."

Shit, "And a million dollars."

"You work for me for a year, and I will transfer a million into your bank account. In the meantime, you work only for me. You may run your yoga studio during daylight as long as you are available after dark."

Well, I sure walked into that one, didn't I? That's the thing about negotiations, you can end up agreeing to something accidentally, and I just agreed to work for a blood-sucking monster.

CHAPTER SEVEN

"You will start tonight. I have a team ready. They will follow you and take care of any rogue vampires you identify. You will live here since your home is no longer safe and Randy will drive you where you need to go. I'll contact my lawyer to draw up the contracts and a realtor to set up some studio viewings. Do you have any questions?"

I sputtered for a moment trying to take in the information dump. The sound of his long fingers tapping on the desk distracted me from my task. Impatient vamp. "You have a team ready?" I ask, "Wait, what happened at my apartment? Who did that?"

He sighed. "That was rogue vampires, they apparently know of you now, and are trying to eliminate you."

"Super. See, even being around you unwillingly gets me a target on my back. How will your team keep me safe from this?" I questioned. "Also, I have a car and can drive myself."

"No, you have a death trap on wheels. Even with repairs, that vehicle is not road worthy, and you are lucky I found you before the rogues did."

Unbelievable.

"The rogues wouldn't have found me if you hadn't been snooping around and left Randy to watch me. You might as well have set up a flashing light on my apartment. And that is a fine car. It never lets me down." Damn hoity vampire. Probably drives a brand-new sports car.

He scratched his forehead with a finger and took a deep breath. I was starting to enjoy stressing him out. It was a bit of passive-aggressive retaliation for all his death threats. No sympathy for super-vamp.

"Ok, fine," he said. "We can compromise. You may have your own vehicle, but you live here. That is non-negotiable. I can't protect you elsewhere."

"There are a lot of vampires here. How do I know I'm safe here?" Locked doors didn't stop him from entering my room. It probably wouldn't stop any of the other vampires here either. I could install a few extra locks. Or maybe an alarm system. With lasers.

"The vampires here won't harm you. Let's not forget the vampire who killed your parents is still free. With your help, we could find him."

I considered his words for a minute. The ridiculous idea of revenge had crossed my mind a few times over the years. I won't deny it. Most of my research had been focused on how to kill them in case I ever saw that vampire again.

"Do you know who did that?" I whispered, taken aback by the turn in our argument.

"Unfortunately, I don't know his name, but I heard about the incident. I can help you track him down."

That wasn't a bad offer, on top of everything else.

"You said I'm not human," I said looking him in the eye. "I want to know why I see you and what I am."

"I will gather all the information we have on your kind and present it to you upon the signing of our agreement."

I narrowed my eyes at him, but he seemed immune to my death glare.

"Do we have a deal?" he held out his hand as if I should shake it, but I just glared at his hand like it would probably eat me.

He sighed and dropped his hand. He could hardly complain when he's the one who purposely tried to scare me into working for him.

"I'll get my lawyer to draw it up," back behind his desk, he straightened some papers that didn't need straightening. I noticed the one on top was similar to the letters I took the first time I was in his house. I was still curious about the letters but needed to find a way to get the ones I borrowed back on his desk before someone found them in my backpack.

I made my escape, and moseyed towards the smell of food, hoping the monsters left me something to eat. I didn't want to sit with a bunch of hungry vampires, but I had skipped a couple of meals now and needed something before I fell over.

The dining hall was nearly empty now. A couple of vampires were still sipping coffee, but the rest had left.

There was an extensive buffet with shiny silver warmers along one wall. At one end was a small stack of plates, so I grabbed one and moved down the table opening and closing the warmers. They contained dinner foods. It made sense since it was evening, but I usually had eggs and toast at this time of day. I grabbed an asparagus stuffed chicken breast and a dinner roll. Close enough.

The food was amazing. I had never eaten such a good meal. The vampires on the far side of the dining hall didn't even glance my way, so I ate in peace. An older woman who appeared to be in her mid-60s came out and took away my plate when I was finished. I thanked her and was glad to see more humans in the house. I grabbed a cup of coffee from the pot on the buffet and went exploring.

The main foyer led to several different wings, the first one I explored had a full gym. My gym paled in comparison to this one. Rubber mats lined the entire floor and mirrors covered every wall. A large open area on one end would have been perfect for yoga practice. The other side had free weights and machines as well as treadmills and stationary bicycles. A couple of vampires were in the room already, so I ducked back out.

At the end of that hall was a large movie theatre. It could comfortably seat thirty people, and the screen rivalled the one at the theatre in the mall eight blocks from my apartment.

When I finished my coffee, I walked back to the dining hall and returned my mug.

As I was leaving, someone called my name. I turned to find a tall, athletic-looking vampire striding down the hall towards me.

"Yes?" I said, taking a step backwards.

He smiled, flashing his sharpies. "My name is Cedric, and I've been assigned leader of Team Lark."

I scowled "It's called Team Lark?"

He just kept smiling at me. Ugh.

"Ok, fine, what's up?" I asked.

"We're meeting in the conference room in twenty minutes."

"And where is the conference room?" I asked.

"North wing, lower level." He turned and walked into the dining room. Great. Which way was north?

After walking around for more than twenty minutes, I found a room set up like a classroom with a small group of vampires seated at desks. Cedric stood at the front of the room. As I walked in, everyone turned to look at me.

I waved awkwardly.

"Now that our Lark has arrived," -he flashed me a toothy grin- "we can start." Cedric cleared his throat. "First, introductions. Lark, this is Gabby, Eric, Tommy and Vlad."

I laughed. Vlad? Really? When Vlad scowled at me, I stopped laughing. "Hi, good to meet you," I muttered.

"So, the plan is to hit some shitty night clubs and round up some rogues. Any questions? No? Great, let's go," Cedric said not leaving any time for my questions. They all stood, and I took a step back. Four massive vampires bearing down on me where I stood by the doorway was intimidating, to say the least.

"Hold on," I said. "Are we just going to wander around in bad areas? That's the plan?"

"Ya, there isn't any other way to do this. We know they frequent nightclubs. That's how they find their meals," Cedric replied.

"And how do you find your meals?" I asked, maybe not wanting the answer.

He smiled that creepy sharp smile. "We have volunteers."

Nope. I did not want to know that. Who in their right mind would want that?

"Let's go," Cedric said, shooing me back out the door. At the end of the hall, we went through a door into a garage. The team of vampires were pumped up and bouncing around as we wound our way to a large van with three rows of seats. Everyone piled in, leaving a place in the second row open for me. That is how I found myself packed into a tin can with a bunch of vamps, hurtling down the highway listening to thunderous classic rock music. I might have wondered if things could get weirder, but I didn't want fate to take it as a challenge.

We pulled into an underground paid parking garage in a depressing neighbourhood. Everyone started getting out, so I slid out too and followed the group through a door into a urine-scented cement staircase. We climbed the stairs and exited through a door at street level. Though we were far from my old apartment now, the dirty streets were the same as the ones I always walked. There were nightclubs and bars all up and down the block, and the team chose one seemingly at random, and we all went in. A band played heavy metal music on a dirty stage, the floors were sticky with what I hoped was beer, and the place was definitely beyond capacity. I bet the health inspectors didn't come here during business hours. The vampires fanned out, leaving me standing alone by the door. Thanks, guys.

At the bar, I ordered a drink. No way was I doing this sober. Turning back to the crowd, I tossed back my drink. Time to find some vamps and get the hell out of here.

I moved towards the dance floor and was looking around for any vampires. Cedric moved up beside me. "Dance," he shouted into my ear. He was dancing, but I didn't feel like joining him. When I ignored his suggestion, he yelled again, "You look suspicious."

He was right, I probably did. So, I started trying to dance to the music, if you could call it music. It was just loud noise with a slight beat. Finally, Cedric just grabbed my hips and made me move. I let him but kept looking around. After an hour, I was tired of dancing and hadn't seen a single vamp except for the ones I had come with.

"Let's move on," Cedric said in my ear, but the whole team must have heard him because they headed for the door too.

Out on the street, I could finally hear myself think again. "That sucked," I said.

"Most nights are like this," Vlad said in a Romanian accent. "Hopefully we do not have to wait for a vamp to drain someone before we catch them, now that you are here." He bumped my shoulder with his and then strode off down the sidewalk.

I scrunched up my face. Heavy metal music and sticky dive bars every night. Gross.

The next club we went into was also packed, but this time with young men and women in tight, bright clothes, some of them couldn't have been over 18. The music was fast dance music, and the bodies gyrated and convulsed like the sea in a storm. There was no way in hell I was doing that, so I sat at the bar, ordered another drink and sipped it slowly, watching people.

And they were. All people, I mean.

When Cedric collected me an hour later, I was feeling discouraged. We walked out of the dance club, and the rest of the team caught up.

"Don't worry. It's only the first night. We will find some soon,"

I was about to reply when a vampire walked out of an alley and headed across the street. I nudged Cedric and pointed with my chin. The team immediately sprang into action. Vlad had the other vampire by the throat in a heartbeat his arms wrapped around the chocking demon so tightly, the muscles in his forearms strained and bulged. Tommy said a quick word into his cell phone as Cedric went back down the alley the vamp had come out of and returned a moment later. A white van with blacked out windows pulled up, the back doors opened from inside, and Vlad forced the other vamp into the back. The van took off and then we were walking back towards the car park.

It was over so fast I was stunned silent. When I found my voice again, I asked: "What just happened?"

"You did your job, and we did our job," Cedric replied.

"Was that a rogue? How do you know he wasn't a good vampire?"

"Every vampire who comes into the city has to present themselves to Mr. Crowden. So, if you see a vampire and we've never met them, they're breaking the law. That particular vampire drained a girl in the alley."

I spun back to look at the alley, but Cedric clamped a hand on my elbow and pulled me along.

"What are you going to do?" I asked.

"Getting you home and then update Mr. Crowden."

"I mean about the girl. Her body?" He didn't reply, just kept tugging me towards the parking lot the van was in. "You can't just leave her there," I said struggling against him now.

"What would you have us do? Call the police and say a vampire bit a girl? People don't believe in vampires, Lark." His radio made a buzzing noise, and he unclipped it from his belt and replied in silent whispers.

I spent the rest of the walk back thinking about the girl who lost her life in the alley. I felt terrible that she was just lying in that dirty alley; surely someone would be missing her. People would be looking for her by morning. I hoped they found her.

Back down the smelly stairwell to the lower level of the parking garage, we climbed into the van. It was only 2 am now, so I wasn't exactly tired, but I had seen enough for one night. I stared out the window considering the way my life had taken a sharp turn in the last week. I couldn't say I was happy about any of it.

At the mansion, I climbed the stairs to my room and locked the door behind me. Then locked myself in the bathroom.

I took out my cell and sent a text to Frankie: This sucks. Want to hang out?

Frankie replied a moment later: I'll pick you up in 20.

I unlocked the bathroom door and went back into the bedroom, hunting through my pile of clothes for something clean to wear. The smell of cigarettes clung to my hair too, but I didn't have time to shower, so I stuck my hair in a pony-tail and changed into semi-clean clothes.

Good enough.

I passed several vampires who nodded or congratulated me. I didn't feel like I had done anything at all, so I just kept walking out the front door and down the driveway to the gatekeeper.

"Hey Lark, good work tonight," the vamp in the gatehouse said as I approached.

"Thanks, I guess." He opened the gates, and I stepped through just as a motorcycle pulled up and stopped. When the biker pulled off his helmet, and I realized it was Frankie, my jaw dropped in disbelief. I had never seen him with a motorcycle before.

Frankie smiled at me and swung off his bike. "I never needed it before," he answered my unasked question.

"This is amazing," I declared. I had never ridden a motorcycle before but had always wanted too.

Frankie took another helmet out of his bag and squished it on my head, doing up the strap before knocking on the top of the helmet with his knuckles. I smiled, and he smiled back at me. He strapped his own helmet on and straddled his bike. He remained standing, waiting for me to join him.

Once I awkwardly climbed on, Frankie sat down and reached back, taking my hands and wrapping them around his stomach. When he started up the bike, the engine was loud, and adrenaline flooded my bloodstream.

As we pulled away from the curb, I tightened my hold on Frankie, and he sped down the street. The rush was amazing and perfect. Frankie took us through the city and past the last street light into the darkness. One headlight cutting through the night. It was cold in the wind, but Frankie's body and the flush of my blood kept me warm enough.

He pulled off the highway onto a dirt track, stopped the motorcycle, and cut the engine. The silence was deafening, and the stars took up the sky like a million drops in an ocean. I hadn't been outside of a city in so long, I had forgotten what it was like out in the country.

Frankie steadied the motorcycle while I slid off. I stumbled but regained my footing. I had no idea how to get the helmet off, but as my fingers raised to the strap to try and figure it out, Frankie's arms came around my shoulders from behind, unsnapped it, and then pulled the helmet off my head. I was glad I had worn my hair tied up because it would have been a total disaster now if I hadn't.

I turned and wrapped my arms around his waist. I sent him a silent thank you as his arms wrapped around me too.

"You're welcome."

"We didn't meet by accident, did we, Frankie?" I had figured it out a while ago but wasn't ready to confront the fact he had manufactured our whole friendship if you could call what we had a friendship.

"I'm sorry," he whispered, "I just wanted to keep track of you at first, but the more I hung around you, the more I wanted to protect you. Keep you safe from the monsters that had stolen your childhood."

"Then why did you let me get involved with them now? Did you tell them where I was?"

"Mr. Crowden found you. He heard your heart rate go up when he sat beside you at Arnie's and knew what you were. If it had been any other vampire, I would have killed him, but Mr. Crowden is cleaning up the city, and with your help, he will get it done. I'm sorry for not telling you the truth long ago."

"It's alright. I knew it was just a matter of time before another vamp found me. Besides, if I can get used to this job, I can do some good with the stupid curse of mine."

He smiled and released me. He pulled a blanket and a glass bottle out of his bag, then took my hand and led me along a narrow path that opened up to a meadow. He laid out the blanket on a hill, and we sat down, he passed me the bottle of rum, and I took a sip. When I offered it back, he refused it. Of course, he was driving. I should probably follow his example if I didn't want to fall off his motorcycle on the highway. Frankie laughed at the thought at the same moment I did. Then I laughed harder at how weird my life had become.

"Tell me about being a warlock," I said, laying back and closing my eyes.

He snorted, "It's not as thrilling as it sounds. I mostly do magic for important people with a lot of money. Boring magic, like making them look younger or be more successful in business."

"Wait, why are you living in our shitty building if you can do magic for rich people?" He bit his lip and looked at the grass. I noticed his cheeks were red, was he embarrassed?

"I didn't live there at first. It was almost two months of pretending before I got an apartment in your building so I could keep an eye on you."

"You creeper!" I laughed. "I can't believe you lived there willingly!" I tore out a handful of grass and threw it at him. He laughed and started picking grass off his clothes.

After an hour, the sun was coming up, and I had a yoga class to get to, so we gathered up the blanket and headed back into the city. Timeout over.

CHAPTER EIGHT

Frankie drove me to the yoga studio and then went across the road to a small coffee shop to wait for me. The class was much better this time. I felt calm and centred after my early morning ride with Frankie.

After class, I double checked the schedule and realized the next self-defence class was that evening which reminded me I hadn't called to quit my job yet and had a shift scheduled tonight. Oops. I called Mr. Fellum. He informed me that my father had already called to let him know I wouldn't be back. He was pretty ticked off but didn't sound all that put out. He probably already had me replaced. Of course, Mr. bossy-vamp had already called. I should have thought of that. Now that my evening was open, I decided I would come back and take the class.

I walked out of the gym and found Frankie leaning against his Motorcycle. The picture of a hot biker with his sunglasses on, boots crossed at the ankles, and arms folded over his chest -- showing off his muscles. It's not like I had never noticed that he was attractive, but now that I had talked to him and he had shown me the place in the meadow, I was seeing him in a new light. I wondered if he had been holding back from me before, or if I had just never bothered to notice; too caught up in my own stuff to see the man in front of me. The really hot man.

He smirked, and I mentally berated myself for my traitorous thoughts.

"Hey," I said as he straightened and held out a helmet for me.

"You ready?" he asked.

When I nodded, he strapped on my helmet and off we went.

He drove through town obeying the speed limit but making fast turns and accelerating quickly after stop lights. It was exhilarating.

I realized there was so much I didn't even know about myself. When I closed myself off from people, I closed myself off from living. I had never tested myself; never imagining that I would like speed and adrenaline. I still wasn't sold on the vampire hunting but riding a motorcycle, and self-defence class were definite improvements to my life.

Frankie pulled up to the vampire house, and the guard slid the gates open. At the house, Frankie cut the engine and stood up to let me off.

"I'll call you tomorrow. Stay safe tonight, Lark."

"Ok, thank you. For today, I mean."

"Anytime, Lark," his serious expression gave his words a deeper meaning, but I wasn't sure what it was.

I turned towards the house and scaled the steps.

Drake held the door open for me at the top of the stairs, and I smiled as I passed through.

"Do you have everything you require, Lark?" He asked, smiling. "If you would like anything in particular stocked in the kitchen or your room, I can ensure that is taken care of."

"Thank you, Drake, I have everything I need. More than everything," I laughed, the house was full of everything I could imagine.

That seemed to please the older man, and he nodded. "Mr. Crowden asked to speak with you. He is in the conference room."

That made me frown. I wasn't looking forward to another encounter with bossy-vamp.

Drake laughed at my expression. "Don't look so glum. He's not as bad as all that."

"That's what people keep saying, but he isn't exactly pleasant to be around or communicate with."

"You will both figure out how to work together soon enough," he said, shutting the door.

"I guess. Thanks, Drake." He just nodded once deeply, and I took the hall to the conference room.

I knocked once and heard the muffled "come" from within, pushed the door open and was greeted by the whole of team Lark.

"Hi, Lark," Cedric said, "How are you doing now?"

"I'm better, thanks."

"Good," Cedric replied pulling another chair up to the table for me. My eyes fell on Mr. Crowden who was scowling. I wondered if he even had a first name. I'd have to ask Frankie. His scowl didn't surprise me. He always seemed grumpy.

"You are supposed to be available to me at night," He said shortly.

"We caught the bad guy, what else do you want from me?"

"I want you to abide by my rules and not go running off in the middle of the night." His tone was serious, but I was not going to let him keep pushing me around.

"I didn't go running off. We were done for the night, so I went out with Frankie. Excuse me if I wanted a little time away." I fell in my seat, exhausted. The sun was up now, and I really needed to get to bed. The rest of the team leaned back in their chairs looking from me back to Mr. Crowden and back to me again like this was the best show they had seen in a long time.

Standing slowly, Mr. Crowden raising his voice slightly, "The rules were clear. You may do as you like during the daylight, but at night you work for me. From now on you will obey the rules, or there will be consequences."

"Fuck you," I stood and tried to walk out of the room, but there was suddenly a solid chest blocking my way. "Move," I said, pushing against the demanding vampire's chest.

He grabbed my arm in his cold, steely hand "I didn't dismiss you," he said in a low, threatening voice

I was done with this garbage. "In case you didn't notice, its daylight, now get out of my way." I spun my arm just as my self-defence instructor had demonstrated. I was stunned for a moment when it worked, but then I zipped past him and strode out of the room, slamming the door behind me.

I was seriously pumped up and grinning from ear to ear at my success in defeating the monster. That is until I found myself suddenly on my back in the hall with a raging vampire pinning me to the ground. His red coloured eyes were as bright as headlights, his glistening teeth had grown to be at least 2 inches long, and his ragged breathing hitched in and out of him with a hiss. He pressed me down to the floor and moved his face down to just an inch from mine.

"Vincent," a male voice spoke softly, stopping the vampires decent towards my jugular. After a moment I realized it was Drake who had spoken. Mr. Crowden pushed away from me, then stood and disappeared, leaving me panting on the floor.

Cedric and the rest of the team came forward, and Cedric offered me a hand. As I stood, he patted me once hard on the back, the way football players might.

"That was a good show, Lark. I don't think I've ever seen him that mad," Cedric said.

"Take this conversation somewhere else," Drake said, shaking his head and walking off down the hall, following the angry vampire.

"Let's go, guys," Gabby said, walking towards the dining room. We all followed behind her, then moved into a line at the buffet. I was exhausted, but eating was a good idea. There were only breakfast foods, so I grabbed some bacon and eggs. I wasn't about to ask them to make me dinner foods when they already made so much food for the vampires.

The team chatted about various jobs and told me stories about some of the hunts they had been on for rogue vampires. I asked just enough questions and made enough comments to be considered part of the conversation, but when they started asking questions about me, I excused myself to get to bed. I had to sleep, unlike vampires and I wanted to make it to the self-defence class tonight.

Back in my room and had a quick shower before falling into bed in a heap.

When my eyes opened again, someone was in my room. "Get out," I yelled, pulling the pillow out from under my head and heaving it towards the invader. The pillow just fell on the floor beside the bed. I never was good at throwing things.

"We need to talk," the ass dared to say to me.

"Then we can talk when it's dark out. It is still daylight, and right now I want to get ready and go to self-defence class so I can learn to kick your vamp ass."

He chuckled. Jerk.

I gave him an evil glare, but he didn't burst into flames, so I threw the blankets back and walked across the room to the large walk-in closet where all my clothes were now carefully hung and folded by some amazing housekeeper that I never saw. I had fallen asleep in my boy shorts and a tank top, so the vamp got a pretty good view of most of me as I walked away, but I was too mad to care.

I put on some yoga pants and a sweater. Pulled on some socks and running shoes and returned to my room to find the vampire had left. Thank God.

I walked down the stairs, and Drake was waiting for me. "I've had your car brought up from the garage," he said.

"Thank you, Drake." I smiled at him and skipped out the door. There, at the bottom of the steps was a brand-new Honda SUV. It was the same original colour as my old Honda, but beyond that, it was not my car.

"Is this a joke?" I asked Drake who was standing at the door.

"No, Mr. Crowden wanted you to have a safe vehicle, so purchased this one for you to drive."

"Where is my car?" I asked, turning back to look at the brand-new vehicle still running quietly.

"I believe it has been turned into a small block of steel by now. Did you know that the brake lines had nearly rusted through and there was a hole in the floor in the back seat?" he asked.

"Ya, but I bought it with my own money. It was my car." I walked down the steps and opened the driver's side door of the new vehicle. It even smelled new. I was a bit sad about my old car, but it had been a death trap. In another year I would have enough money to buy my own vehicle, I'd just have to suck it up till then and drive the damn vampire's car. As long as I had a car, I had some independence.

At the gym, the women's self-defence class was brimming with chittering ladies. The instructor was speaking quietly to some older women, so I did some stretches to get warmed up. My muscles thrummed, eager to release the tension caused by the overbearing vampire.

"Ok, ladies, I would like to introduce you to our dummy," the instructor said, bringing everyone's attention to the front of the room. "This is Ed. He is very well padded as you can see."

The lumbering man waved at us. He seemed to be mostly padding, and I wondered how hard he expected us to hit him.

"Today, we will go through a few possible scenarios. Mainly the attack from behind and the attack from the front by one attacker. As we go through the weeks of class, I have another dummy who will come in and help us with situations where you might have two attackers."

"Let's begin and see how we do. Who wants to go first?" a few women raised their hands, and the instructor went through the procedure of escaping an attack from behind. I was amazed at how hard some of the women kicked and punched poor Ed. I guess the padding wasn't overkill.

"Do you want to practice with the punching bags instead, Lark?" the instructor asked from right beside me.

Ugh, I was hoping she had forgotten my bruised face from last time. "No, I'm ok with this," I said.

When my turn came, I had the pattern of defensive moves down and easily broke free from the dummy. I apologized to him when I shoved him too hard, and he toppled over, but he just laughed and told me it was all part of the gig. Some gig.

Back at the mansion, I pulled up to the front of the house and left the keys in the ignition for the vampire who parked the cars. At the top of the stairs, a vamp held the door open.

"Your presence is requested in the conference room," he said.

"Thanks," I said as I passed by.

Inside the conference room, I expected to see the whole team waiting, but it was Mr. Crowden, Frankie and Drake. I stopped in the doorway. It looked a bit like an intervention. I narrowed my eyes at them.

"Don't look like that, come in and sit down, Lark," Frankie said pulling out a chair for me. Since the vampire was sitting, I sat down too. Frankie took the seat beside me.

"It has been brought to my attention that I may be approaching you and our business together incorrectly," the vampire said.

I snorted and added a sarcastic "you think?"

"Lark, hear him out," Frankie said.

"Why should I?" I asked throwing my chair back and standing. "This was a stupid idea. I shouldn't be working for a vampire anyway. I can't do this job, Frankie!"

Frankie stood, filling my vision and blocking my view of the rest of the room. I tipped forward to rest my forehead on his broad chest. The smell of Frankie - leather and rum - filling my nostrils.

Frankie rubbed my back and rested his chin on the top of my head for a minute. "You can do this, Lark. You did amazing work last night and helped catch a very bad vampire. You can save this city from the monsters who are killing the young women. You just need to work out some things with the monster in this room first."

I snorted a laugh. Mr. Crowden growled, mostly just proving Frankie's point. I took several deep breaths, and when

I straightened away from Frankie, I felt calmer than I had in weeks.

"Alright, fine," I said, "Tell me what you want, vampire."

He sighed "I would like to say that I am used to dealing with vampires. They do not accept authority from anyone except those who can demand it. The only human I have regular contact with is Drake, and he has informed me that humans do not operate the same way as vampires. This is the reason he is employed in our house, so I am taking his word for it and will attempt to address you more gently from this day forward … so long as you obey the rules I have set out."

Drake cleared his throat pointedly.

Mr. Crowden growled. "I will address you without violence from this day forward," he corrected himself.

"Ok," I said.

"Ok? You are supposed to reciprocate my pledge to accommodate you," he said with a sneer.

"Fine, I will try to follow your rules and will make sure I am around at night."

"Excellent," he stood, slapping his hands down on the table, startling all of us "I will summon your team, and you can head out for the night."

Once Mr. Crowden and Drake had left, Frankie pulled my chair around, so I was facing him.

"I heard what happened this morning. If that kind of thing happens again I will fry his ass," he muttered, staring down at his hands.

I laughed, and his eyes met mine, humour flashing in them finally. "Thank you," I said. "For having my back here and being a good friend."

"You got it. Now get to work, so the vampire doesn't have a heart attack."

I laughed again wondering if vampires could have heart attacks and got up, Frankie following behind me. We walked out the front door of the house to find my team standing beside the large van in the driveway. Frankie went to the garage and came back a minute later on his motorcycle. He waved to me and drove out.

"Damn, that's a hot warlock you've got there," Gabby said, elbowing me.

I snorted, "We are just friends."

"He doesn't look at you like he just wants to be friends," she replied.

I was saved from having to continue that conversation by Cedric calling us to get moving.

Time to make friends with the underbelly of the city.

CHAPTER NINE

We drove across the city into my neighbourhood. As we passed Arnie's, I pointed it out, hoping I could solve the mystery of what type of weird mythical being Arnie was, but none of them had ever been to the bar. I should have asked Frankie, but in all the commotion of the last few days, I had forgotten.

We drove past my old apartment building. A for rent sign was in the front door. I missed my old apartment a little. It was small but homey, and it had been mine. Soon someone else would be living in my little attic. I hoped, for their sake, they were short and deaf with a poor sense of smell.

Cedric parked the van in front of a much cleaner nightclub than the ones we had been to yesterday, and we all filed out and past the bouncer. He was a vampire, and I gave the team a not so subtle signal, pointing and mouthing the word 'vampire,' but apparently, we knew him because no chaos ensued. As we entered the club, the upbeat music washed over me and there were a lot of lightly clothed college kids dancing and drinking.

Cedric pushed me towards the dancefloor. I had never gone to college but was the right age to be here – it was full of early twenties men and women dressed casually, like me. I didn't want to dance with Cedric every night, so I tentatively started dancing with a group of girls, and when they didn't shun me, I let myself get lost in the music. I was supposed to be looking for vampires, but instead, I tried to pretend I was just a single college girl with no knowledge of vampires.

My delusion was shattered half an hour later when someone started dancing close behind me. I peeked over my shoulder and quickly pulled a fake smile when I realized it was a vampire. His hands on my hips, we danced for a few minutes. I looked around but didn't see anyone from team Lark.

The vampire whispered in my ear, "Let's get out of here," and wrapped one steely arm around my back, pushing me through the crowd. It was definitely more packed in the club now than when we had arrived. I didn't want to cause a scene in front of the humans, but as we got to the door, there was a different man there. Not a vampire.

I started to panic.

"Actually, my friends are inside. I shouldn't leave them."

"I just want to talk to you for a minute," he smiled. His teeth flashing in the light from a street lamp.

Shit, I was going to die. Where the hell was the team?

He pushed me around the corner into an alley, and I started struggling against him. His grip tightened painfully, and I inhaled to let out a scream, but he covered my mouth with his hand and pushed my face into a wall.

I started kicking, my face scraping painfully on the brick exterior of the building. I felt the monster's teeth slide against my skin and then I was suddenly released and fell to the ground. I spun around on my ass just in time to see my attacker lose his head. Literally.

I lost my lunch and any hope of ever sleeping again.

Vlad was covered in blood. It had sprayed across his face and down his white shirt in a morbid form of art. I vomited one more time before Vlad scooped me up and carried me back to the van, leaving the remains of the vampire in the alley. He put me in a seat and fastened my seatbelt whispering "I'm sorry" repeatedly in his thick accent. My hands were shaking, and I felt like I might be sick again but covered my mouth and forced it to stay down. That was so gross. Vlad got in beside me grabbing a box of wet wipes. He began to clean off his face. He handed me a bottle of water and another box of wipes, and I took a small sip to clear my throat and rubbed the worst of the blood splatters off my face and shaking hands.

"Where were you guys?" I asked unsteadily. My voice hitched with my ragged breath.

Vlad looked guiltily at me then turned his head away. "Gabby thought she saw a vampire take a girl into the restroom. We went to check, but no one was there. By the time we got back, you were gone. I'm so sorry, Lark."

I liked Vlad; he was very fatherly, but these vampires couldn't protect me. I knew they couldn't, and still, I put my trust in them. I should always go with my gut; it had kept me safe this long.

"It's not your fault," I muttered despite my brain screaming it's all their fault. My stomach was still churning, and my mind was fuzzy. I just wanted to go home and take 60 showers.

The rest of the team piled into the vehicle silently, Cedric was the first to speak once we were moving.

"That won't happen again, Lark," he promised.

I just muttered a reply, eyes firmly on the city outside the window. He took out his phone, spoke into it silently for a moment, and then set it on the dashboard.

Nobody spoke until we got back to the house. Mr. Crowden waited on the porch, fire blazing in his eyes. There was a string of muttered curses from the team at the sight of him. If I thought he was mad before, I was mistaken. He looked like he was ready to lop off some heads.

The team slowly got out and moved around to the front of the vehicle, but I stayed put. I was not in any shape to deal with his anger issues. Through the window, his eyes locked on mine and slowly drained back to the usual vamp colour.

When he spun on his heel and went into the house, I saw the shoulders of most of the team members' drop-in relief. I guess they were waiting for him to explode too.

I climbed out and stumbled up to my room. I started stripping as I walked towards the shower. I flipped on the water as my tears started and my breathing hitched. Now that I was alone, fear and pain overtook me.

I slid down to the floor in the shower and let it all out. I had almost died. I could still feel the monster's teeth scrape my neck. The side of my face where that brick had scratched me was tender, and I gently fingered the scratches as the water washed away my tears.

When my breathing returned to normal, I stood on wobbly legs and washed my hair twice before harshly scrubbing the rest of my body with soap until my skin was red. I stepped out of the shower and wrapped myself in a thick robe.

I knew he was there, sitting in the shadow of my room, but I didn't say anything to him. I just went into the walk-in closet and got dressed in clean, soft jogging pants and a big hoodie sweater. I pulled my wet hair up into a ponytail and tucked it into the hood of my sweater then went out to face the monster in the corner.

"I'm sorry," he said in a soft voice. I almost didn't hear it because he was so quiet.

"Ok," I replied, confused. Where did the angry vampire on the porch go?

I curled up on the bed, under the heavy comforter. He didn't seem interested in yelling at me, so we sat in silence for a while. I wasn't tired, too wound up still, but laying in the big bed helped me come to terms with what I had seen. Beyond almost being killed by the monster, what Vlad had done so easily terrified me too.

Vlad had saved my life, but the casual violence was not something I was used to. The world of vampires was a brutal, bloody world. I had already known vampires were killers and even if these vampires weren't out to kill humans, they still hunted and killed.

"I would like to show you something," he said finally, startling me out of my dark musing.

I slid off the bed and put on some socks and shoes then stood to wait for him. He frowned a moment and gestured for me to follow him.

He led me to the main floor gym. A few vampires lifted weights in the far side, but Mr. Crowden led me to the mats. Once there, he grabbed my wrist. His hand fit around it a steely grip, and I jerked back, but before I could panic, he spoke again, "You already know how to get out of this hold."

His voice was so stern that it shocked my memory.

I did exactly what I had learned in self-defense, and I escaped his control. I had forgotten it when I really needed it – in the alley with a vamp about to drain me.

"Do it again," he said sternly, grabbing my wrist.

We did this a dozen or so more times until I was doing it quickly and effortlessly, though my wrist was red and sore.

"You will train with your team every night for the next month," he said, his usual bossy tone returning. "I have the information you requested about your heritage. You may collect it from my office. In the morning, I have a real estate agent prepared to show you some studios that may be suitable for your business." As he left, I sighed heavily. Twice. Taking a break from dirty night clubs sounded great. Training with the team sounded like it might be good too. I needed to learn to fight back since I couldn't run from my problems anymore.

First, it was time to learn something about myself. Why I was cursed? Maybe even how to undo that curse?

At Mr. Crowden's office, I knocked gently on the door. A moment later, the vampire himself opened the door, speaking a strange language into his cell phone. He handed me a file folder before closing the door again. Not that I expected a polite conversation, but really?

Back in my room, I started reading through the papers. Most of the documents were photocopied information about vampires. They look like they had been taken straight from a textbook. There was information about their strength and speed, what they ate, where they lived. It was everything I had been looking for all my life, but everything I had already figured out from being around them these last few days, except for one piece of vital information I didn't know.

To kill a vampire, his spine must be severed, or head completely removed. No mucking about with stakes, no sunlight or crosses. That was it. I had no idea how I was supposed to do that, but the next piece of information I came across was the most important to me.

One human would be possessed by Durga, the mother goddess and consort of the Hindu God, Shiva. She would bestow them with the sight so that they could do her work. The blood of the vampires would bring Durga forward, making the human she has chosen faster and stronger than average and giving them one singular desire – to destroy evil vampires.

Those demons who killed indiscriminately, the ones who were out for nothing but themselves – they were Durga's target and would be hunted and destroyed.

The Durga and her chosen one would work seamlessly to maintain the balance.

I was freaking possessed by some Hindu deity? How the fuck did I get rid of her? This was insane. There was no other information. Nothing that said how to undo whatever it was this Durga had done to me, but I was pretty sure I didn't want to be possessed.

On top of that news, 'Hunted and destroyed' didn't sound like something I was likely to be up for. Maybe I could just let Vlad and the team do the hunting and destroying. They seemed to like that. Although the speed and strength stuff would be super great, I wasn't looking forward to being possessed.

I put the paper back in the folder and stuffed the whole thing away in the bottom of my sock drawer, like that would stop whatever shit was about to hit the fan.

I was not currently stronger or faster than anyone above the age of five. I had never trained to fight, but I had been training in yoga for many years, would my apparent superpowers not have shown themselves already? Superpower yoga? I snorted. Ok, maybe not. That was the end of the information though, and I still had many questions. Well, if this was true, and I assumed it was since Mr. Crowden didn't seem the type to perpetuate myths, that meant I was supposed to, someday be possessed by some creepy spirit and be able to kill vampires. Let's not forget the only way to kill them was to sever their spines. Gross.

It was nearly morning, I had yoga first thing, and then I would go out with the real estate agent, so for good measure, I took another shower, got dressed in clean clothes and put the night behind me.

I had breakfast in the dining room with the vampires. Most of them now knew who I was and waved or said hello. It was still hard to interact with them but getting easier to look at their smiling faces and not see vicious teeth wanting to rip out my throat. I shivered at the thought and filled my plate.

I ate quickly and hustled out the front door of the mansion. I had forgotten to ask Drake to bring my vehicle up, but that didn't matter because Frankie was sitting on his motorcycle at the bottom of the steps.

"Hey," I said as I approached.

"Hey, yourself. I heard you almost got eaten last night." He frowned at the scrapes and light bruising on my cheek. I had tried to hide the marks with makeup but wasn't very successful.

"Almost. Not quite." He snorted a laugh and got on his motorcycle, waiting for me to get on behind him. As we sped down the driveway, all thoughts of vampires cleared out of my mind as the rush of speed and comfort of Frankie's presence took their place.

Frankie let me off at the yoga studio and then crossed the road to the coffee shop.

Inside the gym, the muscle-bound man at the desk shook his head when he saw the scrapes on my face. I rolled my eyes and went to the locker room to leave my wallet and cell.

Shanti started the class, working us through some of the poses we had learned this session. Today's class was a great distraction from the last twelve hours. I felt calmer and almost hit deep meditation at the end.

"Great job today, Lark," Shanti said as I was rolling up my mat and getting ready to leave.

"Thanks," I replied, "It was a great class."

She smiled. "I hope you will stop in to visit us once you have your studio open."

"How did you hear about that? I haven't even purchased a studio yet."

"Your father called to say you wouldn't be able to teach the beginner classes here anymore because of work commitments but mentioned you would have your own studio closer to home soon."

I snorted; that pushy bastard, and why did he always introduce himself as my father? Creepy. "That's true, but I do plan to keep coming to your class, I have more to learn."

She laughed. "You could easily teach my class. You are too hard on yourself. I'm glad to hear you will still come around though. You have such great energy."

"Thank you, I'll see you next time," I said as I took out my phone and threw an angry text rant at the bossy vamp who had just cancelled my beginner yoga classes. I loved those classes, and now I would probably never see the hockey kids or the old sweethearts again. Mr. Crowden probably had the agent showing me places much closer to his side of town, and I doubted any of my current students would want to drive across town for yoga.

I sighed.

Outside, there was no sign of Frankie but right at the curb was the Tesla driving vamp, Randy.

"Hey Randy, what happened to Frankie?" I asked, sliding into the shiny little coop.

"He had to go deal with some magic stuff. Those warlocks are a strange bunch."

I laughed and said, "And you vampires are super normal, right?"

He bit his lip and looked a bit abashed. "I guess we are pretty odd too."

Randy drove me to the other side of town, as I predicted, and we met with a real estate agent at an old studio that had been vacant for several years, judging by the grime on the floors, walls and windows. The front windows were huge. The space had high ceilings and was airy and bright, and there was ample open green space behind the building where I could offer outdoor classes on nice days. The building needed quite a bit of work and elbow grease to bring it up to code and make it shine, but I knew it was the perfect place right away. It was exactly what I imagined in my mind when I dreamed of my own studio.

The agent insisted I see the other locations, though, so we drove around town and saw four more. None had the same feeling as the first, so I made the agent take me back there again, now even more confident that it was the perfect place.

I stood in the large open room that would be my yoga studio and imagined little old grandmas and hockey kids and single ladies and moms and tots. All the different classes I would offer and all the smiling faces of the people I would help. I turned towards the front door and imagined where the front desk would be for registrations and information. Someone could work for me during the day. I could have an employee.

I turned back to look at the back wall where I could have mirrors to help beginners find the right poses and with daydreams all floating through my mind. I didn't even notice the new presence until he spoke.

"This is the one you have chosen then?" Mr. Crowden asked.

I jumped, completely caught off guard, and turning towards him I nodded, giving him a grin.

"Very well. It will need some repairs and updating, but Randy will be at your disposal. He can organize contractors during the day and will update you on the progress in the evening."

"Ok," I said, going back to my daydreaming.

"Lark," he interrupted again. The agent and Randy had already left, and Mr. Crowden was holding the door for me. I didn't want to go, but I was getting tired now and needed to get some sleep. I followed the vampire out into the daylight and slid into Randy's Tesla.

Randy shook me awake a few minutes later, and I climbed the stairs, collapsing on my bed and falling to sleep for another day with the plans for my new studio swirling through my head.

CHAPTER TEN

"Oof" the wind was knocked out of me for a second time, and I gasped like a fish trying to reclaim my lung function. In my mind, I used every colourful word I could remember to curse the blood-sucking jerks!

"Sorry, Lark," Gabby said, again.

This was the third night. They were trying to teach me to fight, but mostly it was just a bunch of vampires repeatedly knocking me down. The only thing I was learning was my lungs would start working again before I passed out. The panic was still real, every time.

"I've never tried to teach a human to fight before," she complained. She had already said this several times. Apparently, she had a slow learning curve.

I still couldn't speak, so I just shook my head at her and kept gasping. My eyes watered, blurring my vision, but I knew who had just walked in when the rest of the vampires shut up and stood quietly looking at their feet, trying not to provoke the already angry vamp.

"Why do you people keep damaging the Durga? Are you completely incompetent?" he growled, and team Lark backed up a few more steps.

I would have loved to express my feelings about him calling me the Durga, but I was starting to think I was going to pass out this time. The room was hazy, and darkness decreased my vision as the angry red-eyed vamp leaned over me.

"Stop falling down," he said helpfully as he grabbed me under my arms and lifted me to my feet. The action seemed to kick start my lungs again, and I took a huge gulping breath, finally filling my neglected airways.

"Why didn't I … think of that," I gasped.

He frowned. "I've had enough of this..."

"You and me both," I interjected.

"… I have found you a proper instructor," he declared. "He will arrive tomorrow night. For now, you can take the rest of the night off."

Excellent. I limped out of the gym and towards the front door of the house. I wanted to see my studio anyway. The sale had closed the day after I told the agent and Mr. Crowden that it was the one I wanted.

At the door, I started to ask Drake to bring my car up, but Mr. Crowden calling my name stopped me.

"I assume you are going to see the studio. I have to go and sign some papers in that neighbourhood anyway. I'll give you a ride."

Stuck in a car with the grumpy vampire didn't sound like fun, but as it was only a few minutes away, I could probably manage it.

"Alright," I said cautiously. When I hadn't seen him for the last two nights, I assumed he was off travelling somewhere until he popped up in the gym just now.

"Don't look so concerned. It's just a ride in a car."

Hmm, guess I'm not good at hiding my emotions.

Drake had brought the boss vamp's car up. It was a very sporty BMW. I knew it would be.

He drove fast too, which I wasn't wholly opposed to, and we made it to the studio in record time. I hopped out, thanked him, and he took off down the street.

Randy held the door open for me. He had already done a lot of cleaning in the reception area. The front windows were beautifully clear now. Some contractors had started tearing up the old linoleum floor while others had begun remodelling the bathrooms and locker rooms. I had chosen the paint colours for the walls and had hired an artist to do a mural of a sunset on the inside front wall, surrounding the windows. The outside was going to get new vinyl siding and a large sign that read Sun Down Yoga, the business name I had chosen years ago.

I sat on a paint can and admired the space. It was amazing to think that in a few short weeks I could be doing classes here. Randy had gone back to painting the newly built reception desk. I couldn't believe how hard that vampire worked. Not needing to sleep made for excellent productivity.

When Randy finished the second coat, he put the lid back on the paint and sat beside me.

"Thank you for helping with this," I said indicating the whole room.

"I'm glad to be able to help. I'm not much use to Mr. Crowden, so having this project has been wonderful."

"What do you mean, not much use?"

He rubbed his face. "I shouldn't have said it that way. It's just that he only really has jobs for warriors. I am not much of a fighter, so I mostly get in the way."

"That's ridiculous! Not everyone can fight monsters. You have a great talent for organizing. Look at what you have done here."

His cheeks pinked slightly. "Thank you, Lark, but vampires aren't supposed to be interior designers or project managers."

"Well, you are a vampire and an excellent interior designer and project manager. I bet there are other vampires just like you who wish they could be doing more creative things." I don't know when I developed this 'vamps are people too' attitude, but my righteous indignation at the non-inclusive nature of vampire culture was strong.

Randy laughed. "Maybe we can start a trend. A be-the-best-vamp-you-can-be, kind of thing."

I joined his laughter until the doorbell chimed, and the boss walked in. Randy's laughter stopped abruptly, and I rolled my eyes.

"Working hard, I see," he said snidely.

"Just taking a break to admire the work that's already been done," I replied in the same tone.

Mr. Crowden narrowed his eyes but didn't say anything more. He scanned the room and nodded. "Very well, are you ready to go home? The sun will be up in an hour."

I stood up slowly and dusted my pants. I was looking forward to having breakfast, a hot bath, and heading to bed. My back and various other parts of me hurt from all the recent combat training.

I followed the vampire out the door and climbed into his speedy little car.

"You know, Lark, I'm not as harsh as you think," he said as he pulled the car away from the curb.

I stifled my laugh as best I could, but he heard it. "Sorry," I muttered, forcing my face into a serious expression.

He was silent a long time as if I had messed up the talk he was planning to have with me, and now he had nothing to say. Oops.

When we pulled up to the house, I moved to get out, but he stopped me with a cold hand on my arm.

"Call me Vincent, Lark." He released me and slipped out of the vehicle, unfolding his tall frame and marching into the house before I could reply. Alright then.

In the dining room, I found my team sitting down with their breakfast, so I filled a plate and sat down beside Vlad.

He smiled at me, nudging me with his shoulder. I smiled back and started eating while listening to the conversation already going on between the team.

"I'm not saying that all rogues are bad," Cedric continued. "Just that the rogues in this city should be exterminated. They cause too many problems for the rest of us."

"I disagree," Gabby countered. "I think each case should be looked at separately. Some vampires just want to be left alone and not be part of the community, that doesn't make them inherently bad. Vampires not breaking the laws should be left in peace."

"You always say that, but we both know that vampires can't be left in peace, eventually they decide to start causing problems if they aren't kept in line. Look at Vernon. He was left alone because everyone thought he was obeying the laws. Now we know the truth," Cedric said before going back to his food as if that settled the argument.

"Who is Vernon?" I asked.

Vlad turned to me and spoke, "One of the elders, like Vincent."

"And Vlad," Cedric interjected happily.

Vlad growled and continued, "Vernon was allowed to move to a small village but ended up going crazy and killing all the humans."

"Jesus," I whispered.

Vlad gave me a sad smile. "That's what happens when we don't live in communities. It's called the Fall. No vampire has ever returned to sanity once they have Fallen."

"Is that why we hunt down all the rogues?" I asked.

"And the Fallen, yes. We can't allow the humans to discover us and mass slaughter is like a flashing light pointed right at vampires."

I sat back, thinking about his words. If this was true, if the vampires went crazy, I needed to be out there, hunting. Ever since I had read the information about my heritage, I had felt a stronger urge to go out at night. Even with the fear of the monsters in the dark, something was pushing me forward. My brain whispered 'Durga,' but I stomped that down.

"Did you catch Vernon?" I asked.

"No, he fell off the radar but now and then we hear about a mass murder in a different country. We fly in, but always too late and he is long gone," Vlad finished sadly.

"Anyway, no more bedtime stories, we have to get to work, and you have to get to bed. Your new trainer will arrive tonight, and you better be in top form," Vlad said before he picked up my empty plate, along with his own, and walking them back to the kitchen.

I said my goodbyes and dragged myself back to my room. Food coma here I come. After a shower, I slipped into fleece pyjamas then tucked myself in and fell asleep.

***

"Again," the bossy bastard said from the side of the gym where he had been standing for the last two hours yelling at me.

"Damn it," I cursed before getting back up and stretching out the kink in my neck. This new trainer was human but didn't have much better plans for me than my team had. I was on my ass more than anything and definitely not learning how to fight.

I got ready for my next assault, bracing my legs in a wide stance. We had been practicing how to escape from a rear attack, but the attack never came; instead, I heard an 'oof' and spun around to find the assistant, also a human, on his back and a very angry vampire, standing over him.

"What the? Mr. Crowden, that wasn't called for, he's just doing as he's told," I said, looking down at the poor guy on the ground. The air was knocked out of him, and I totally felt for the guy.

"Vincent," the vampire said, "I asked you to call me Vincent."

"Fine, Vin-cent," I drew his name out. "What the fuck?"

"This instructor came highly recommended but doesn't seem to have any clue how to teach someone to fight. I've had enough of this. I will train you from now on. This is too important to trust to these imbeciles."

The instructor was quite red in the face and looked like he might yell but, thankfully, Vlad ushered him out the door before he could start yelling and get the vampire angrier.

I kept my mouth shut. I wasn't looking forward to spending one on one time fighting the grumpy vampire, but I needed to learn to protect myself.

Vincent took a deep breath and collected himself then turned to me. "We will start tomorrow night. You can take the rest of the night off."

I waited until his back was turned to do a little happy dance. I hadn't seen Frankie in days and hadn't had a night at the bar in longer.

I jogged back to my room and sent a text to Frankie who agreed to pick me up.

I had a quick shower and changed into jeans and a tank top, then hopped back down the stairs and out the front door.

As I strapped my helmet on, I happened to glance back at the mansion and saw the curtains close on Vincent's third-floor office. Had he been watching me?

"I'm glad you messaged me, Lark," Frankie said bringing me back from my musing.

I smiled up at him. "I can't believe I have a night off. Where do you want to go?"

One corner of his lip lifted in a grin. "I know just the place."

Frankie and I rode out of the city and into the next town. He pulled the bike up to a one-story, board and baton building that looked like an old-fashioned saloon except for the dozens of motorcycles out front instead of horses.

"What is this place?" I asked as I took off my helmet.

"This," he said proudly. "Is the Crossroads."

I laughed, "That's what it says on the back of your jacket."

"Yes, it's the name of our coven," he replied.

I stopped. "Are you sure I should be here? Isn't this kind of a secret?"

Frankie reached back and grabbed my hand, pulling me forward till he could wrap his arm across my shoulders. "You will be fine. I decide who can come here." He laughed and walked me through the door.

Inside, as I suspected, everyone stopped what they were doing and looked at me. Most had curious faces, but some seemed less than pleased.

"This is the Durga, anyone who has a problem with her being here, speak now so I can fry your ass," Frankie said.

"Can you really fry people?" I whispered.

He winked but didn't answer my question. I let the fact he called me Durga go. It kind of sounded badass.

Most people in the bar chuckled and went back to what they were doing, but a couple of people still looked pissed. I had never seen Frankie this relaxed and care-free before. He was always quiet and broody when we were at Arnie's. Which reminded me...

"What is Arnie?" I asked.

Frankie sputtered a bit on the drink he had just taken a sip of, then wiped his mouth and laughed again.

"I knew you would pick up on that at some point. He's a warlock too, but an ancient one. He is probably a couple hundred years old, well into retirement age.

Huh. I had no idea that warlocks lived so long. Arnie looked to be retirement age, so I guessed they just aged slower than humans. I started to wonder how old Frankie was, but he beat me to it.

"I'm thirty-five," he replied to my unasked question. He looked about twenty, so that confirmed my theory.

The bartender handed me a drink, and we sat quietly for a while. I listened to various conversations between the men and women in the bar. Or I should say witches and warlocks. It seemed this was a place for all things magic because some people were practicing magic in the corner, lighting and extinguishing a candle with their minds or whatever. Some men beside me were discussing the best way to make a vanishing spell.

"Listen, you have to do it this way, or you will blow up the whole block," one of the men down the bar bellowed to the man next to him.

"Calm down, Len," Frankie called over to the irate man.

"I'm just trying to keep this fool from killing himself and everyone around him," Len called back.

Frankie shook his head. "I'll be right back, Lark," he said as he slid off his bar stool and crossed to the disagreeing men.

I sighed and took another sip of my drink. When I set my glass down a thin, blond woman sat beside me and looked me up and down.

"So, you're Frankie's girl?" she asked with a smile.

"Uh, we are friends," I replied.

She laughed, and the sound tinkled through my eardrums making my teeth hurt.

"So, you aren't together?" she smiled.

"No."

"Cindy, are you harassing Lark?" Frankie asked frowning at the woman.

"Not at all," she smiled standing a setting her hand possessively on Frankie's chest. "I was just getting to know your friend." She looked down at me like I was an adorable small child.

I snorted at her petting Frankie's chest like she was a cat in heat, rubbing herself on him.

Frankie disentangled himself from her, sat in his seat beside me and downed his drink. He raised two fingers to the bartender who promptly delivered another drink. When Cindy finally wandered off, he downed his second drink and said, "Let's dance."

"Uhm. Ok," I replied. I had gotten pretty good at dancing in the clubs we had been going too. Not great, but good enough.

It turned out that Frankie was a great dancer. I had never seen him do much more than drink and shoot pool, so it was a complete shock. After a few songs, we both loosened up, and Frankie's hands on my hips tightened, bringing us closer together.

Cindy's eyes flashed with anger from across the room where she sat with a group of witches before she looked away. Jealousy was not something I had experienced before. Most people didn't even notice me, much less have a reason to stare daggers at me.

Frankie picked up on my thoughts and looked behind him at Cindy.

"She has been chasing me since we were kids," he said, leaning in close to me. "Witches can be pretty determined."

I snorted, and we continued dancing until I was getting tired and sober. At the bar, I had another drink, but Frankie's limit was apparently two drinks, saying that he had to drive me home at some point and didn't want to kill me. I appreciated the thought.

After meeting a few other warlocks from the coven who were strangely 'happy to finally meet me,' I started to feel like this was a date, and I was the only one who didn't know. I blocked the thought from my mind as soon as it entered because, if it wasn't, I didn't want to embarrass myself around the thought-reading warlock. Frankie led me back out into the night. It had cooled off a lot since we had gone in and I shivered in my tank top.

Frankie took off his leather jacket and slid it over my shoulders. It was huge on me, but heavy and warm. Then he strapped my helmet on my head, pausing for a second and looking at me.

"What is it?" I asked, unsure why he was staring at me so seriously. I thought he was about to say something. Then he turned and put on his own helmet before getting on the bike and holding it up for me to scramble on behind him.

I wrapped my arms around his waist, and he kicked the engine on and tore out of the parking lot of the clubhouse.

Frankie took turns fast and straights even faster. The rush was incredible and snapped me out of my energy lull. He drove me back to the mansion and through the gates. The only trouble with the motorcycle was that we couldn't talk, and I was left to wonder what it was he had wanted to tell me in the parking lot.

At the steps to the house, he stood up and let me off but didn't turn off the motorcycle. I took off my helmet and handed it back to him. He tucked it away and smiled at me once sadly before driving off.

Just as he disappeared out the driveway, I remembered I was wearing his jacket, but it was too late to return it. He was already   gone.

CHAPTER ELEVEN

It wasn't quite daybreak, but the house never slept. The vampires were always coming and going. I had no idea what most of them did, though many seemed to have jobs in the community. I knew one was a banker because I had been introduced to him when he set up my new account and credit card. Vincent supplied one to each member of the household to cover expenses and incidentals. I had yet to find a reason to use either. Another was the lawyer who had drafted our agreement. Vincent had offered to get a different lawyer to handle our business, but the contract was so basic even I could understand it. Most of it.

I returned to my room and hung up Frankie's jacket, so I wouldn't get it dirty, then remembered those stupid letters still tucked in my laptop.

I took them out, folded them up and stuffed them in my back pocket. Following the halls around the building, I passed a few vampires heading to the dining room for breakfast.

I knocked on the door to Vincent's office. When there was no sound from inside, I slipped in and shut the door behind me. The office lights were off, and only a trace of light came under the door and through the open window blinds. I circled the desk and pulled the pages out of my pocket before flattening them out on the flat surface. They were crinkled, but I thought if I put them at the bottom of the pile of pages in a desk drawer maybe he wouldn't notice. I tucked them away, and my eye caught on a pile of letters. I picked it up the stack and tried to get a bit of light on the top sheet from the window.

"Find what you are looking for yet?" He asked, startling me, making me drop the pages to the floor. I bent down to pick them up, scrambling for something to say.

"I was just..." I couldn't think of anything.

"You were just what? Exchanging the letters you stole from my desk for some new ones?"

I stood up, holding the gathered pages and he was right in front of me. I tried to take a step back, but the desk was behind me.

"I was just..." I really had to get better at lying.

"I know what you were doing. Would you like me to read this out loud for you?" he asked, snatching the pages from my hands.

"No, I'm sorry. I just thought..."

"Yes, you just thought all vampires were like the one who killed your family. You judge us all by the actions of one vampire. As you have always done. As you will continue to do until you finally get your head out of the sand and look around you. Nobody is here to hurt you. We are not your enemy." He slapped the pages down on the desk and walked out of the room.

I stood in shock for a minute, I had seen him mad and raging before, but this was new. His face hadn't contorted, eyes weren't bright red, and teeth weren't long and scary. This was like he was disappointed. Crap. I was such an ass. I mean, he had threatened me at first, but since then he hadn't given me any reason not to trust him.

Feeling about two feet tall, I walked back to my room and flopped down on my bed. I had no time to sulk though. I had missed too many of my yoga classes and had to get going. I changed quickly and met Drake in the foyer.

"I have your vehicle out front for you. I hope you have a good class." He smiled. I faked a smile back and thanked him.

Shanti led us through various poses, but my mind kept straying to the vampire, and I had trouble keeping my breathing steady. Yoga used to help my life be centered, but now it seemed that my life was just messing up my yoga.

At the end of class, Shanti pulled me aside.

"Are you ok, Lark?" she asked quietly.

"Yes, I'm just distracted. I'll do better next class," I replied.

"You know, some things are too big for yoga. Maybe some extra meditation will help you. I'm sure it's stressful opening your own studio."

I only wished that was my biggest worry right now. I wished I had someone like Shanti to talk to about the vampires and warlocks and drama of my life. She was the closest thing I had ever had to a female friend, but she knew nothing about me or the world I was wrapped up in.

"Thank you. I'll try that," I said, and slapped on a fake smile even though I doubted that meditation would help.

When I walked out of the building it was pouring rain and Vincent's sporty little car was in the space my SUV had been parked in. As I approached, I realized that the man himself was in the driver's seat. He put the window down a crack.

"What are you doing? Where is my car?" I asked.

"I had Drake take your vehicle home. I would like to speak with you. Get in." He raised the window, so I couldn't argue with him. Since it was raining, I didn't think about it too long. I sighed and opened the door, sliding into the leather seat.

"What did you want to talk about?" I asked, trying to cut the nervousness that was fogging up my corner of the car.

He didn't reply right away; instead, he seemed intent on driving his vehicle carefully through the parking lot and out onto the main road.

I sat back and watched the world go by. The city was alive during the day. Commuters drove like maniacs, in and out of traffic and pedestrians with brightly coloured umbrellas hustled to where they had to be. I rarely got to see the world this time of day because I was always so tired and just trying to get home to bed after Yoga. On the rare occasions I did notice the day time world, I was amazed at the vibrant colours and fast movement.

I was having trouble fighting off the sleep that tried to pull me under and eventually the gentle motion of the car lulled me, and I started to doze a bit. I must have fallen asleep because my eyes shot open at the sound of the car door slamming I looked up to find we were in a cemetery.

"What the hell?" I muttered as I hurried out of the vehicle. At least the rain had stopped. Vincent had already started walking away from the car and deeper into the cemetery.

I wasn't sure I wanted to follow a vampire through there, but my better judgement was still asleep. His long strides were still taking him farther away from me, so I jogged to catch up.

"What are we doing here?" I asked as I finally came up beside him.

He noticed me jogging and slowed his pace. "You will see," was his only reply.

As we crested the hill near what I thought was the back of the cemetery, I noticed the gravestones continued but looked older. They were cracked and covered in moss. Some were so worn by time, they were smooth and could no longer be read.

When we reached the bottom of the slope, Vincent continued into the trees. The loamy scent made my nose itch, and the soft ground was difficult to walk through. It seemed to pull the last of the energy out of my legs, and I was barely shuffling along under the giant old-growth canopy. My eyes were heavy now too, with the sun rising into the sky.

"Shit," I cursed as I tripped over a root and almost fell to my knees. "What are you ... oof," I gasped as the vampire scooped me up and started carrying me through the forest.

"I can walk," I complained.

"Evidence suggests the contrary."

"That's not funny. It's daytime. I should be in bed."

"It's not much further," he replied, flaring his nostrils. "You still smell like the warlock."

"Don't sniff me, you weirdo. And what's not much farther?"

Then the trees opened up and before us was a small rotting cabin. The roof looked like it was barely hanging on and it had more moss than walls.

"Did you bring me here to kill me?" I asked half serious.

He grimaced at me. "Will you ever believe I don't intend to kill you?" he asked with a heavy sigh.

"I was just joking," I said, before muttering "mostly."

He shook his head and set my feet back down on the overgrown, weedy ground.

"This," he said with a flourish, "is the first house I lived in when I came to the new land. America."

"Holy shit," I said walking towards the humble old shack.

"I was one of the first of my kind to come here. Vlad followed shortly after."

"Why are you showing me this?" I asked, turning around to face him.

"Because I want you to know me. To know that I was once like you; in a new world and trying to find my way. This land was overrun with witches and warlocks. We had no treaty in place, and it was hazardous for my kind, but Vlad and I persevered and made a life here. We called a truce with our enemies. You can do that, too. Your new life will be better with us. It will be more."

I wasn't sure when he got all philosophical, but his words did strike a chord with me. I had sometimes allowed myself to dream of a better life. One where I wasn't lonely all the time. One where I wasn't afraid to get close to people.

A life I could actually live.

After a moment, I nodded silently. The rawness of the moment hit me, closing my throat so I couldn't speak. No one had ever given me hope before. If he was offering me a better way, a safe way, how could I turn that down? I had already accepted his job offer. Signed the lawyer's paperwork. But I understood what he was asking of me. He wanted me to accept this new life. Accept him.

For the first time, he didn't look like a monster. He still had bright glowing eyes and rows of pointed teeth, but his humanity was showing too.

"Good, now come along. I plan to start your training in four hours. You human types need some sleep, I suppose." He turned and marched off back the way we came, leaving me behind.

So much for his humanity showing.

***

"You aren't even trying!" he yelled at me while I lay there dying. Ok, maybe I wasn't dying.

I groaned, rolled onto my side and pushed up to my hands and knees.

"I've only had four hours sleep," I moaned.

"This level of incompetence cannot be blamed on lack of sleep."

"Argh, you are such an asshole," I whimpered, struggling to my feet. Apparently, there was no way to teach me to fight without knocking me down… a lot.

"This time, if you could not trip over your own feet and actually attack me, that would be appreciated."

I grumbled and got into the fighting stance he had taught me. I moved forward quickly, swinging my fist at his head before aiming my foot at his solar plexus. Both missed him, but I was still on my feet, so I spun quickly and punched again. Every other time he had come up behind me when he zoomed out of the way of my attack. This time was no different, so when I let my arm blindly lash out, I caught him right in his solid square jaw.

"Shit, shit, shit!" I screamed holding my hand. I looked down at it and almost passed out at the bloody mangled mess my hand had become. "Oh God, I'm going to puke," I wailed, running from the mats towards the bathroom in the far corner. I made it in time, just barely, and collapsed, losing all my dinner.

"Are you finished?" the bastard asked.

"Look at what your face did to my hand!" I hollered, holding up the injured appendage for his inspection.

He gently wrapped a towel around it. Probably just to keep it from bleeding on the floor. Bits of broken bone had penetrated the skin on the back of my hand. I had never seen something so disgusting in all my life. It hardly even resembled a hand anymore. Once it was wrapped in the towel, I could no longer see it, but I could feel the awkward way the tendons sagged, and the bones scraped. It turned my stomach again, but I swallowed steadfastly and tucked my wrapped hand into the crook of my other arm. Denying my brain access to the images that were probably etched on the backs of my eyeballs was all I could do.

"You will probably live. Come on, I will get you healed up, so we can continue," the idiot replied.

I pushed off the floor, thankful that I had tied my hair up before we began and now didn't have any vomit in it. My hand was throbbing, and when I stood up, I felt a bit dizzy. The asshole took hold of my good arm and helped me out of the bathroom. He led me across the gym. All the other vampires who had been pretending to work out, so they could watch me get my ass kicked, again, turned back to their machines and weights as Vincent's eyes swept across the room.

"Where are we even going?" I asked as we passed the front door and headed up the stairs "I need to go to the hospital."

He just kept pulling me up the stairs and around to the third floor. I had never been up that far but hoped he had some magic to fix me as he seemed to suggest. I was probably going to pass out soon, and I couldn't feel my fingers anymore. The swelling was setting in.

At the top of the stairs, he took a left and pulled me through a doorway. Inside, the bedroom was large with a double set of doors on the far side that led out to a balcony. The bed was an extravagant four poster with red silk sheets and an excessive number of pillows. Besides the bed, there was an armchair in one corner, and several shelves lined the walls, full of old books. Everything was immaculate, and I realized this was probably Vincent's own bedroom.

"Why am I here?" I asked.

He spun around to face me. "You are here because I am going to heal your hand and then you will learn how to punch without breaking your hand."

"Do vampires have magic or something? How are you…? Ugh, never mind. Just fix it. I'm going to pass out." The edges of my vision turned black as he settled me down into the chair. Just as my eyes closed, I swear I saw the vampire lick my hand. That jerk.

I am not an appetizer.

CHAPTER TWELVE

Where the hell am I?

Daylight was streaming through the huge double patio doors as I sat up and rubbed my eyes, vaguely recognizing the red sheets and the bookcases along the walls. Then it all came flooding back. The room, the fighting, the broken hand, the vampire licking me. Gross. Vamp drool.

I held up my arm and admired my fully healed hand. I could probably put up with a little vamp tongue action if it meant I wouldn't be disfigured the rest of my life. Angry voices echoed from outside the door. One I recognized as the hoity vamp himself. The other sounded like Frankie, and he was pissed.

"I told you not to hurt her or I would fry you," the warlock hollered.

"And I told you," the vampire countered, "she punched me and broke her own hand. I have already healed her, and she is resting. She is perfectly fine. You have no reason to be concerned."

"Please, gentleman, perhaps you would take this discussion to the office," Drake interjected.

The arguing continued but moved away from the bedroom door, so I lay back down and held my hand up to inspect it again. Not even a scar remained. It was like it never happened. My eyelids were heavy still, and the sun through the window was blinding, but I pushed the covers off and stood. My shoes had been taken off, but I still wore my bloody jeans and shirt. Thankfully, black didn't stain, but the blood had crusted, leaving my clothes feeling hard and scratchy.

I opened the door and peeked out. Nobody was around, so I walked to my room, quickly stripped, and threw myself in the shower. I scrubbed off the reminder of what I had done to myself.

Fresh and in clean clothes, I walked down the stairs towards the office.

"Thank god you are up," Cedric said from behind me. "I thought your warlock was going to turn Vincent into a toad."

I spun around to face the team leader. "He's not my warlock," I said, irritated by the implication. "Are they still in the office?"

"Guess your super hearing hasn't kicked in yet?"

"Super hearing?" I asked, confused.

"Ya, Durga's get improved hearing. Didn't anyone tell you? Cedric asked.

"I knew I would get faster and stronger. I didn't know I would get other bonuses, but I guess it hasn't kicked in yet."

He laughed, "Well they are still in the office and still mad. In fact, I think Vincent is madder now. I'm not sure which one of them would win in a fight. It's like Superman versus Batman."

"For fuck's sake," I muttered under my breath, hustling towards the office. These two were going to give me grey hairs with this crap. I pushed the door open without knocking.

"For the sake of the treaty, you better hope to God she is in one piece," Frankie finished.

"You mean me?" I asked innocently.

Vincent straightened, his eyes falling on me. Frankie spun on his heel and poofed across the room, appearing in front of me so suddenly I almost fell backwards. He caught my shoulders, holding me upright and inspecting me like I was a piece of fine china that had been dropped on the floor.

"I'm fine, Frankie. I just hurt my hand on the vampire's hard old head," I snickered trying to bring the tension in the room down to a reasonable level.

He finally looked me in the eye, apparently satisfied with my appearance. He didn't say anything for a long minute then he pulled me into his arms and hugged me. It still felt foreign and uncomfortable when he held me, but after a moment I relaxed and accepted it. I hadn't had a real hug in years.

"That's terrible," Frankie whispered, plucking the embarrassing thought right out of my head. Great.

"Are you satisfied now, warlock?" Vincent growled. As Frankie released me, I looked past him to the vampire whose eyes were shining bright red.

"Just be more careful till her powers come in. She is basically human still," Frankie warned before he hugged me again, holding me longer than he needed to before walking out the door.

My eyes met Vincent's, and I watched as his eyes slowly drained of red.

"We will try again after dinner tonight. You should get more sleep," he said, picking up his pen and scratching notes on a piece of paper.

"Alright," I muttered as I turned and left his office.

I found myself in the dining room without really meaning to go there. I was lost in thought about the vampire, the warlock and my missing Hindu deity with my superpowers. I wanted to be faster and stronger. Who wouldn't? If they made me strong enough to fight a vampire, I wanted them right now.

The dining room was nearly at full capacity. It was lunch time, and I had never visited at this time of day. Everyone apparently gathered together at noon. I grabbed a sandwich and drink and squished in between Gabby and Vlad at the table with the rest of the team.

"How are things going?" I asked. Then I noticed they all looked a bit unhappy.

"Fine," Gabby muttered. "We just aren't having much luck finding the rogue vamp that has been killing people down by the waterfront." She ran her fingers through her hair and sighed heavily. I started feeling guilty. My ability to see the vampires wasn't doing anyone any good locked up in this house.

"We got spoiled the two days we had you out with us," Vlad said, smiling at me.

"I'll be ready to go soon," I promised. Maybe I could take a stroll down by the docks tonight and see what I could see.

***

"Absolutely not."

I shouldn't have asked for permission.

"Oh, come on, Vincent," I begged from my seat across the desk from him that evening. "People are dying. I could go, have a look around at the docks, and be back with plenty of time to train."

"Yes, and more humans will die if you go off and get yourself killed before you are strong enough to fight the rogue vampires. We have already seen what little you can do when confronted with a raging vampire, so until you figure out how to keep yourself alive or find the powers of the Goddess, you will stay protected."

"I would be protected. I could stay with the team and look around," I protested.

"Last time that didn't work out for you. Why would you want to go back out there?"

I looked around the office trying to come up with a reason that didn't sound crazy. I felt crazy. Apart from honestly wanting to help, something was pushing me towards those docks; I could feel it trying to shove me out the door.

I kept biting my lip. I didn't want to sound foolish. I was a tiny girl who had taken a couple of self-defence classes and been knocked around by some vampires for the last week. I still hadn't seen any sign of these supernatural powers everyone seemed to think I would have. Ugh.

"Are you suicidal?" Vincent asked, seriously. "Having lived a very long time, I understand that feeling, but you have a bright future to look forward to."

"God, no, I'm not suicidal. I want to help, and I think I can without getting killed. If I'm careful and stick close to the team, I can make a difference. I'm supposed to be doing that, right?"

He stared at me for a moment. I assumed he was weighing the risk against the rewards. He seemed the type to consider all possibilities before acting.

"Alright, you may go out for one hour and look around. You will not wander off from your team. You will stay within arm's reach of Vlad the whole time."

"OK," I said, jumping from my seat and exiting the office before he could change his mind. I travelled down the halls and stairways until I finally found my team in their meeting room discussing the night's strategy.

"I'm in," I said. "Boss says I can go out for an hour as long as I stay close to you guys."

"Awesome," Gabby said.

"We won't let you get eaten, Lark," Vlad added.

Cedric stood and straightened his jacket before speaking, "Alright team, lets head out."

Everyone stood, and we headed for the garage.

Gabby hadn't stopped texting since we left the conference room.

The ride through the city to the docks took forever. Traffic was jam-packed, and we hit every red light on the way. The people leaving the hockey stadium were boisterous and revelling; the home team must have won.

By the time we parked, I was starting to regret my enthusiasm to come out tonight. The push to come had lessened now that I was here, and it was so sketchy. There were very few street lights and a lot of people hanging around. It was mostly homeless people, setting up camp for the night. At daybreak, the police cars made a sweep through and kicked out anyone still loitering here, but at night they never seemed to bother with this area of the city.

Though a large number of homeless people populated the area, they were mostly transients and kept to themselves. I could see how a vampire would have an easy time picking them off.

Gabby finally tucked her phone away and looked up, opening the door to the van and letting us out the side door.

"Alright, kiddo, if the boss says we have you for one hour then we better get you home on time," Cedric said.

I nodded and moved with the team across the parking lot towards the water. The docks were a massive series of shipping ports that stand high above the shoreline. The shore was rocky and not good for swimming, but the docks provided decent cover and kept the people safe from the elements. As we scaled down the embankment, we could see most of the homeless people were jammed in a tight space near the top of the embankment, where the ground meets the dock. It gave the best protection from the elements, and they were hidden from view there.

Vlad stepped up beside me as I stumbled down the rocky bank. He offered me his arm like in the old-fashioned movies with ladies in petticoats and men in top hats. I tucked my hand under his arm and rested it on the inside of his elbow, steadying myself on the uneven surface. At the bottom was a flat overgrown weedy strip of land before another drop off into the dark water. There were well-worn paths through this area, making walking easier.

I let go of Vlad and started glancing at faces. They were mostly what you would expect, older men with greying beards and balding heads. Some were muttering to themselves or ranting. There were a few small groups of men and women who huddled around small fires, but there were also families. Moms, dads and kids in sleeping bags, lined up like rows of dolls on a shelf. I didn't like to think that some children grew up like this, without a safe place to sleep or to call home. My life may not have been great, but I always had a roof over my head and a door that locked.

I continued my search for vampires. When we reached the far end of the docks, we turned around and moved back the way we came. Scanning the faces produced no one of interest, and I grew frustrated when my hour was up, and I still hadn't found a single vampire. I didn't want the children out here, unprotected.

"Oof," I heard behind me. I spun around and let out a scream as a group of vampires descended on us. Vlad was beside me in the next breath. He scooped me up. Holding me to his chest, he sprinted down the packed earth path faster than I had ever moved.

The stop was sudden and jarring when Vlad ran straight into another vampire. I tumbled along the ground several feet, scraping and scratching my skin on the ground. I came to rest flat on my back in the dirt and looked up to find a vampire I had never met standing over me hissing like an angry cat. He reeked of copper pennies and death. He reached down and grabbed my hair, pulling my head back to expose the soft expanse of my jugular.

He reared back to strike, but the monster was ripped away, pulling out some of my hair in the process. Vlad produced an ungodly roar. I looked up in time to watch Vlad twist the monster's head off with his hands. His signature move.

That sudden violence didn't end the fighting as six more vampires descended upon us, tearing and biting at Vlad in an attempt to get to me. Other members of our team appeared amid the struggle, assisting Vlad. A long knife flashed and then another. Blood sprayed the parched ground like water from a hose, and one by one they destroyed the rogue vampires.

I shoved off the ground, wincing. Vlad appeared in front of me, checking my injuries. A sharp pain stabbed my side when I took a breath, possibly a cracked rib, and there were scrapes on the palms of my hands. I couldn't find any other injuries.

"Where is the rest of the team?" Vlad asked.

"Eric was killed before we even knew it was an ambush and Gabby … disappeared," Cedric answered, shaking his head.

"Eric is dead?" I hadn't spent any time with Eric, and he seemed shy. But he must have been a strong vampire to be on the team.

"Gabby disappeared?" Vlad questioned.

Cedric just nodded, biting his lip. Cedric may have been the team leader, but Vlad's true place in vampire hierarchy was evident at this moment. He was older than the rest of the vampires except maybe Vincent.

"This was a setup," Vlad muttered as he turned us back towards the van, taking my arm and pulling me up the embankment. He was moving too fast for me to keep up and I tripped hard before he noticed. I cut my knee on a rock, and he cursed, scooping me up and setting my feet down on the asphalt.

"I'm sorry, Lark," he muttered unhappily. "That old bastard is going to throttle me."

"It wasn't your fault. Do you think Gabby was abducted?" I asked, wondering how she disappeared.

Vlad laughed without humour "No, I think she finally jumped ship. She has been talking more and more about how the rogues should have rights. We should have seen this coming."

"But you guys are a team. She wouldn't send a bunch of rogue vampires to attack you." I recalled the conversation they had in the dining room. About the rogues and how she thought they should be allowed to live. There was a big gap between thinking rogues should live and thinking we should die.

"Oh, kiddo, I had almost forgotten what it's like to be young and naïve," Vlad scoffed gently.

I immediately felt like I was six years old again, and maybe to Vlad, I was. But I still had a hard time believing Gabby, who had eaten with us just at lunchtime, concocted a plan to get the whole team killed.

Maybe I was naïve.

Back at the van, we all piled in and drove silently back to the mansion. I was covered in vampire blood again.

Cedric pulled out his phone and spoke silently into it before tucking it back in his pocket. His face looked paler than ever, and I assumed he had called Vincent. The vampire was probably not too pleased.

I watched the city go by out the window, letting my mind wander to my past – to the family I had lost and the many people I had met. I wondered how Mr. Fellum was doing at the Discount Emporium and if someone had rented my old apartment.

I longed for the days when my biggest concern was that my car might not start, or my rent might be late. Those thoughts turned back to Gabby and her betrayal. Eric's needless death. I didn't even feel fear as I thought I should. I felt anger, rage.

My breath started coming in and out fast and heavy. The injustice of this world bit at me with fangs sharper than a vampire's. The humans had no one to protect them from the violent beings who roamed the shadows and took their lives without thought. The fury built until it poured out of my mouth with a deafening scream.

I strained against the seat belt that held me solid to my seat until I heard metal groan. The van came to a stop, and panicked voices started speaking rapidly. I couldn't even hear them over the thrum of my pulse in my ears. I slammed sideways, knocking the van door open. Steely arms circled me, but I pushed them off and spun to face my attacker.

"Calm yourself, Lark," the vampire who had ruined my peaceful existence commanded.

I flew across the pavement slamming into him and smashing him against the side of the van. My rage knew no bounds, and my wrath would be swift and brutal.

"Demon!" I yelled, but my voice didn't sound like my own. It sounded harsh and violent.

I threw a fist at the vampire's head, but he disappeared, and my punch went through the van window. The glass shattered and cut open my arm up to my elbow, the bright red blood that sprung from my ruined skin brought me back to reality. I stood staring at my arm as if it were a foreign limb somehow attached to my body. The pain felt distant somehow like it was irrelevant.

Maybe I was dreaming.

CHAPTER THIRTEEN

"You aren't dreaming."

I turned towards the voice. Frankie.

"Then … how did you get here?" I asked him, not quite sure what I was even asking.

"I came just now when Vincent summoned me. It seems you stumbled on Durga's powers and tried to knock Vincent's head off," he replied, looking just a bit too pleased to report my actions.

I looked over at the vampire. "He ruined my life."

Frankie laughed. "Was it so great to begin with, Lark?"

No, he was right. Vincent didn't ruin my life. Vampires did. I shook my head trying to clear my thoughts.

"I need to sit down, Frankie."

Frankie walked over and took my hand, the one that wasn't bleeding freely, helping me up the front steps to the mansion. At least we made it home before I lost control of myself. All the vampires scattered as we entered. In fact, when I glanced behind me, the team and Vincent had abandoned the front yard. Scattered like leaves on the wind.

"Where did everyone go?" I asked

"An out of control, Durga doesn't give a vampire a warm and fuzzy feeling. I'm sure once you calm down, they will be fine."

I snorted. "The vampires are afraid of me?"

Frankie led me through my bedroom door and across to my bed where he sat me down and kneeled in front of me.

"You just almost killed the oldest vampire in this corner of the country, maybe the world. Vampires are the top of the food chain," he replied while untying my muddy shoes.

"Jesus," I muttered.

The vampires were afraid of me.

"Why did I attack Vincent?" I mumbled mostly to myself, but Frankie answered.

"Have you met him? He's a bit of an ass," Frankie laughed as he stood me up and led me to the bathroom. He sat me up on the counter and turned on the taps in the sink. He gathered a washcloth and some tweezers and started cleaning my arm. Bits of glass were embedded in my skin, but the bleeding had stopped already. As Frankie plucked the bits of glass out, I realized that my information packet on Durga was sorely light on factoids about my new powers. I watched my skin close up almost as soon as each piece of glass was removed, leaving whole fresh skin without a trace of a scar.

"Holy shit," I whispered.

"That comes in handy when you put your fist through a sheet of glass, huh?" He smiled up at me.

Our eyes locked. His smile slowly fading, he reached up and wrapped his hand behind my neck, weaving his fingers through my hair. He leaned forward, his lips touched mine tentatively and then more firmly before breaking away.

He turned his head to the side. "Sorry," he muttered and then he disappeared. Just like that, poof, he was gone.

My long-standing assumption of Frankie's gender preferences was apparently misguided.

I shook my head and smiled at the lingering feel his lips on mine. After a few moments replaying our interactions for the last few weeks. I wanted to thump myself for being dense.

I had no idea why he apologized though or disappeared for that matter, but all the glass was out of my arm, so I shook off the weird feeling that I was missing something. Had I thought something strange while he was kissing me? I tried to remember what I was thinking, but I was drawing a blank, so I just flicked on the shower and started prying myself out of my dirty, bloodstained clothes. This was becoming a habit.

The hot water melted the stress away as it washed away the layers of caked grime. My ribs felt fine now, and although I was missing a small patch of hair from the vampire at the docks, my scalp didn't hurt either.

Scrubbed clean, I tossed on some yoga pants and a tank top and moved back into my bedroom. Shanti had suggested some meditation and now seemed like a good time.

I turned off the lights and sat cross-legged on the floor at the foot of the bed, facing the window that looked out over the backyard of the mansion. There were no lights on back there, but I could just make out the tree line in the distance and the place where the black of the trees met the dark blue of the night sky. I looked at that place until I could make out the branches and leaves. They suddenly became startlingly clear, and I closed my eyes to shut out the sudden new capability.

I rested my hands on my knees and shut down all my senses. Letting my mind drift away from any coherent thought. I had always been good at meditating before vampires came into my life; shutting down and blocking out was easy for me.

It was connecting with people that I found impossible.

That was the last thought I had before drifting off to sleep.

I was in a temple. The ceiling was painted in ornate gold leaf, and the walls and floor were white sandstone. The wind blew through the open parapet, raking sand across my skin. I was sitting in Lotus Position on the floor in the center of the room, but I was not alone. In front of me sat Shiva. The third Hindu god.

His posture matched my own, his knuckles resting on the floor, palms forward, legs crossed, and eyes shut. His long tangled black hair swayed slightly in the breeze, but the rest of him was perfectly still.

I took a long moment and soaked in his full appearance. His light, nearly translucent skin and animal pelt clothes. The cobra that circled his neck like a deadly decoration and the white ash smeared across his forehead, partially covering his closed third eye.

His eyes flashed open. "Durga."

Then he was gone, and my eyes opened to the new pink sky.

"Where did you go?"

Startled out of my peaceful moment, I turned my head to find Vincent sitting in the armchair in the shadows of my room.

I didn't know how to reply to his question, so I just stared. Dressed in all black, his neatly pressed slacks and dress shirt were a perfect match. He had one leg crossed over the other, and his index finger rubbed across his chin in thought. I hadn't really looked at him before, beyond a cursory glance. Sharp teeth – check. Glowing eyes – check. If you looked past that, he was just a man. A man I had tried to kill only hours ago.

"I'm sorry," I apologized before looking back out the window. I remembered in the haze thinking he had ruined my peaceful life, but it hadn't been peaceful. It had been painful. I had been afraid all the time. I didn't know what my life was now, but it wasn't worse.

"You ready to get to work?" he asked softly.

I kept my eyes trained out the window, pulling in a deep breath through my nose and uncrossing my legs, stretching them straight out in front of me before letting go of the breath. I stood up and turned towards the door.

"Let's do this, fang face," I said as I walked out the door.

His chuckle behind me felt good. Like we had finally found common ground.

"Fuck," I muttered from the gym floor. I might be stronger and faster than I used to be, but I was still ending up on my ass a lot. Good thing I now had super special healing abilities too.

Being fast and strong also doesn't help if you don't know how to punch or kick without breaking yourself.

"You are improving," Vincent said with way too much humour.

I flipped him off as my knuckle crunched and popped back into the correct position. At least his nose was doing the same thing. He didn't seem bothered by it or the blood running down his chin.

"How am I supposed to take out vampires if I can't do enough damage to kill you?" I asked narrowing my eyes at him. He didn't seem bothered by my suggested death threat either.

"You will learn to use a knife when you're ready, but weapons can be taken away from you."

I leapt to my feet and charged the bloodsucker. He dodged as I spun to follow him, but he was already on the other side of the room, I pushed myself towards him and caught the back of his shirt. He spun quickly flinging me off and into the wall of the gym. The wet thud of my sweaty body hitting the wall rang through the room, but I wasn't deterred. The pain was distant, and I was starting to understand that this was part of my new power. In the middle of a fight, I could ignore everything else.

Maybe my alter ego Durga blocked it out. I felt the urge to fight now. I hadn't felt that before. I felt powerful.

We had already been fighting for a few hours, and I was getting tired. The sun was up, but it felt so good to be strong, fast and nearly invincible, I didn't want to stop.

I ricocheted off the floor, leaping across the room to tackle Vincent, but he stepped aside as I got close and only my arm caught him. I wouldn't be taken down by his spin this time. I clamped both hands to his arm and rode out his deflect then pushed hard off the floor, getting the height I needed to knock the vampire off his feet. As he crashed to the ground, I rode him down, straddling him where he lay panting on the floor. Victorious, I raised my hands to the sky and flung my head back.

That was my mistake because he just flipped us over, pinning my arms to the ground and grazing his teeth across my jugular.

"You're dead," he whispered in my ear.

I felt goose bumps rise on my arms and legs and the hair at the back of my neck stand on end. My breathing was already ragged, but I felt a hitch at his voice in my ear.

He stood up pulling me up with him, keeping my body flush with his until we were both on our feet, then he let me go and took a step back.

As soon as his eyes left mine, the sounds of the room filled my ears again, reminding me that most of the vampires were in the gym lifting weights or running on treadmills in an attempt to watch the show without being obvious. I rolled my eyes. Bunch of nosey assholes.

I retreated to my room and had a long hot shower before slipping on an oversized t-shirt and sliding into bed. It was full daylight, and I hadn't had breakfast, but I was too tired to stagger back downstairs. I had hoped that my new-found magical superpowers would allow me to stay awake during the day like an average person, but it wasn't meant to be.

***

That evening I woke earlier than usual, meaning I had gotten less sleep than usual, but I didn't feel tired, so I grabbed a quick meal and drove over to check on my studio remodel.

When I pulled up the contractors were just pulling out, and Randy waved happily from the doorway. I couldn't believe how much he was enjoying taking care of the work on the studio. He seemed to thrive on organizing. I returned his wave as I parked my SUV.

"You will not believe what the contractors have done in the locker rooms," he gushed, "They are so talented."

I found it hard to believe that contractors could do that much to amaze me, but as I walked in, I saw precisely what Randy had been talking about.

Heavily frosted glass partitioned the shower stalls, white marble coloured lockers covered two walls with built-in benches in a cream colour, and the floor was tiled to match.

The dispersed lighting left the place seemingly warm despite the hard surfaces everywhere.

The men's locker room was similar except in more of a masculine grey tone. I couldn't believe my studio had locker rooms. The central area was still in shambles of ladders and boxes of supplies. Wires hung from the unfinished ceiling but having one part done felt amazing. As I returned to the main area with Randy, the artist I had hired to do the mural h just finished packing up her paints and waved as she walked out.

The mural only had a small corner of the art painted, but I could see the design now that she had laid out in pencil. It was going to be perfect. I couldn't wait.

I walked to the middle of the open area, stepping over boxes and tools until I was in the center in a small clear space among the carnage and chaos. I sat down on the dusty floor and crossed my legs. Resting my hands on my knees, I closed my eyes and let my mind go blank. It was so peaceful here despite the chaos of the construction and the dust. Quiet. Clearing out the negativity and doubt, I let myself float away.

When my eyes opened again, I found Vincent crouched in front of me.

"What are you doing here?" I asked

"Where did you go?" he asked, his eyes like laser beams, holding me in place. I wasn't used to anyone seeing me. Not the way he was looking at me now. Most people just glanced at me or looked for a second. This was like he was trying to puzzle me out.

"I don't understand your question," I replied, honestly hoping it would tone down his intensity, but he just looked at me harder.

"When you do that, you disappear. I mean, you are still sitting there, but it's not you anymore. You are somewhere else."

"That doesn't make any sense." I stood up and dusted the dirt off my pants.

"Wait, please?" he said standing up too

He sounded so vulnerable that I stopped and looked back at him.

"I was meditating. I didn't go anywhere. I just shut off my brain for a bit. It helps me relax and focus."

He nodded, and I swear he was going to keep asking me questions, but instead he turned to Randy.

"I trust that you are keeping track of all the necessary contractors?" Vincent said harshly to the smaller vampire.

"Of course, Mr. Crowden. They are all working very hard and doing top notch work."

"Very well. Let's go, Lark, we have training to get to. It's dark out now." With that, he marched out the door. I said my goodbyes to Randy and walked out too. My SUV was suspiciously missing, but I was getting used to the bossy vampire stealing my vehicle when he had something he wanted to talk to me about, so I just slid into his little sports car as he revved the engine and took off towards home.

CHAPTER FOURTEEN

Things were just starting to get bloody in the gym a week later when Frankie's angry voice rolled in through the open doors.

"You better pray she's not injured," he hollered, before appearing magically between me and Vincent where we had paused our sparring at the sound of his yelling.

"Who the hell are you shouting at?" I asked Frankie. His eyes swept over me as he drank in my appearance. My sports bra and tight workout shorts didn't cover any of the blood smears from the minor scrapes I'd received tonight. It was becoming a game of who would bleed first. Me or the vampire I was fighting. My skills were developing fast, and I was starting to worry I might hurt Vincent.

"What has he done?" he asked, more to himself.

I answered him anyway, "He hasn't done much, look at him," I snickered, making the vampire growl. He already had a bloody lip and two broken fingers as well as scratches across his neck. If I had been armed he would be dead, I was sure of it.

Frankie grabbed my hand and pulled me towards the door.

"What are you doing?" I asked. The vampires parted like the red sea for the irate warlock. I realized I could hear his heartbeat pounding fast as he dragged me along. My hearing has improved a lot in the last couple days, but it still caught me by surprise.

"I'm getting you the hell out of here. I told him not to hurt you. He's lucky I haven't turned him into a bat."

I snorted a laugh. Fighting made me a bit drunk on adrenaline, and with Durga blocking the pain and stealing my common sense, I was having a hard time taking the moment seriously. I spun my arm, breaking out of his grip, and he grabbed me again harder this time, pinching my skin. I slammed the fist of my free arm down on his arm, breaking his hold and nearly breaking his arm, then shoved him hard enough that he hit the wall in the foyer with a thud before sliding to the ground.

"What the hell, Lark?" he yelled from where he had landed on the floor.

"You don't control me." It sounded like my voice, but I swear I couldn't stop it from speaking. "I am the consort of Shiva, and you will not control me. I am more powerful then you can imagine." A wicked thought occurred to me, something I had been right on the edge of piecing together for the last week,

"Did you know I would be powerful, warlock? Did you know this was how my life could be, and instead of helping me, you left me scared and alone and powerless all that time?" my voice had risen to the point that the nosey vampires who had followed us out of the gym started to back off and skitter away. Only Vincent held his ground.

Frankie didn't reply at first, just sat on the floor holding his arm, staring at me like I had two heads.

"I'm sorry," he finally muttered just before he vanished.

A bubble burst from within me, and the deity was gone, leaving me to deal with the fallout of what had just come out of my mouth.

I turned and ran to my room, slamming the door behind me. Fuck. Fuckity fuck.

That was the only word in my vocabulary for a while. I tidied my room. Found some cleaning supplies and scrubbed my bathroom. Hung up some clothes and folded some socks. Made the bed and dusted the furniture. When I was finally out of things to distract me, I collapsed on the bed and cried.

Frankie had been the only constant in my life before coming here. He had protected me. Hadn't he? My stupid mouth and the cranky old deity were going to ruin my life. Even if what I said was true, he probably didn't purposely try to hurt me. God knows I didn't want to meet any vampires before being forced to come to this house. Crap. He had feelings for me, and I probably had feelings for him too, and now it was all just ruined.

I had to make this right. It wasn't past midnight yet. I could text him, but that seemed like a cheat. I was sure he wasn't living at the old building anymore, but I could probably remember the way to the biker bar he had taken me to. Maybe he would be there.

I got changed into clean clothes and splashed water on my face. In the foyer, Drake was standing at the door.

"Do you want me to bring your car up?" he said, picking up the phone beside the door.

"Yes, please, Drake. Thanks."

I walked out the door and sat down on the steps.

"You don't owe him anything," Vincent's voice echoed from the veranda behind me.

"Maybe not, but I'm not an asshole, Vincent, and that was an asshole thing to say to someone who cares about me. He was trying to protect me."

"You don't need protection anymore, Lark."

I turned to look at him, but he was gone.

As the mechanic employed by Vincent slid out of my SUV in front of the house, I hopped in and put it back in gear.

There were dozens of motorcycles in front of the clubhouse. I couldn't tell if one of them was Frankie's, but I hoped I would find him in there.

As soon as I walked through the doors, all the conversations dropped off. Heads swung to look at me, some still curious, others still angered by my presence, including one pair of steely grey eyes belonging to a blond bimbo. Cindy still had a problem with me.

She swaggered over and stopped in front of me.

"You shouldn't be here," she said with a sneer. "He doesn't want to see you."

"I came to apologize, not that it's any of your business," I said, trying to push past her.

"He doesn't care. You should leave before I make all your hair fall out and your skin turn green."

"Cindy, shut up," Frankie said as he walked out of the back room.

Cindy scoffed before walking past me, close enough to bump me hard with her shoulder and continuing out the front door of the bar.

"Um, can we talk?" I asked, suddenly nervous now and considering just turning and running out.

He snorted a laugh, probably reading my thought and motioned me into the back room I hadn't noticed the last time we were here.

Past the doors was a cozy office. It wasn't expensive like Vincent's, but it was clean and tidy, and photos covered the walls. Pictures of men and women on motorcycles or gathered around, arms hooked over each other's shoulders and bright smiles on their faces. They all wore jackets like Frankie's.

I inspected the pictures, trying to figure out what I was going to say. Even though I could feel his eyes burning into the back of my head, I didn't want to turn around and see his anger or rejection.

"That is my father and his enforcers," he whispered from right behind me.

I bit my lip and turned to face him. He didn't look mad.

"I'm not mad, Lark, how could I be mad, when what you said was true? I was selfish and stupid. I wanted to keep you safe and out of danger. I wanted you to have the life you wanted – a normal life." He rubbed his hands through his hair. "Maybe because I wanted a normal life too."

"We were never just normal, Frankie," I said.

He laughed like I hoped he would. He had said the same words to me when all this change started.

I sobered, "I'm sorry," I whispered, resting my hand on his chest and biting my lip.

His eyes bore into mine with so much intensity that I couldn't look away. He brought his hand up and ran his thumb over my lip, stopping me from chewing on it, then he leaned in and claimed my lips with his and pressed his body into mine. His arms wrapped around my back like he would never let me go. I didn't want this moment to end.

He backed away slightly and said, "You forget how to knock?"

I was confused for a second and was about to ask him what he was talking about, but then I heard another voice reply: "I was just bringing you a drink, I didn't realize she was still here," Cindy intoned from the doorway.

Frankie moved away from me taking all the heat in the room with him. I shivered and looked up to find Cindy's dumb face scowling at me.

As Frankie turned to look at her, she slapped a pretty smile on her face and said, "It doesn't matter what wild oats you sow, we are betrothed. It's only a matter of time before we are married."

As Frankie turned back towards his desk, Cindy briefly glared at me with a smug look on her face.

I waited for Frankie to deny this ridiculous claim, but the bastard wouldn't even look at me. I saw red. I could easily grab her and rip her smug head off her shoulders, all I had to do was…

"Lark," Frankie said softly, startling me out of my visions of violence.

"I'm going to go, I have to get back to training," I lied before hustling out the door of his office. I wanted to stop and have a few drinks but thought better of it and headed for home. It's not like Frankie and I were in a relationship, but for him to kiss me when he is practically married to someone else was so wrong.

Back inside the mansion, cheering was coming from the entertainment room, echoing through the foyer. I peeked in the doorway to find most of the vampires watching a hockey game. It was a bit weird, but I guess even monsters like the good old hockey game.

I didn't follow any sports, but they had the bar in the corner flowing, so I joined them for a little while.

Stumbling back to my room early that morning was funny. Maybe only to me, since I was the only one giggling, but funny none the less.

I finally figured out how to open my door, and I landed in a heap on the bed. I kicked my boots off and crawled forward till my face smushed down in a pillow. It was so fluffy, I raised my head and let it fall back into the pillow one more time.

"Are you intoxicated?" the boring vampire asked me.

"Are you intoxicated?" I mimicked in my snootiest voice before giggling again.

"What is the matter with you?"

"Where should I even begin?" I asked, exasperated with my life in general. "I have serious trust issues, chronic guilt and I'm too short to shop in the women's section of the department stores. I have to buy all my clothes in the children's section." I splatted back into my pillow before mumbling "Also, I just made out with a guy who is going to marry the evil witch of the south-west."

"I didn't catch that last part," he replied, his voice much closer than it had been.

I sat up and turned towards the vampire "I made out with Frankie and then found out he's apparently betrothed to that witch, Cindy."

Vincent snorted, "Are they still participating in that barbaric tradition? Mating the strongest of their kind together like they are running a zoo. They say we are set in our ways…" he muttered on like that for a while longer, but I stopped listening.

"Lark, come spar with me," Vincent said, pulling me out of my misery.

"I'm drunk," I complained.

"You can still fight."

Ugh. I dragged myself up. Hitting someone would make me feel better, and since there were no witches or warlocks handy, a super durable vampire would do. Drunk Lark was the crazy ass deity too.

The gym was empty and when we entered Vincent turned the lock keeping everyone out. That was a good plan cause if I puked up all that vodka I drank, I didn't need witnesses.

I did a few stretches and took off my shoes. We both sparred barefoot to minimize the injuries. Broken bones put a damper on the fun. I turned back to Vincent who had taken his shirt off. His chest was covered in tattoos. I wasn't expecting it, having never seen him with his shirt off before and his personality didn't suggest he was the type to have tattoos. I stared a bit too long, and he smirked. Jerk.

"Alright, let's go," I said.

I circled to the right, and he went left, waiting for me to make the first move. Such a gentleman. I stepped in fast and popped him in the nose, the satisfying crunch soothed some of the night's drama, but not nearly enough.

"Why do you always have to bloody my face?" he asked, sounding irritated like he didn't know the answer. It was the blood. I had put it together a few days ago. Durga craved it, and it made my power kick into high gear. I didn't question her on this. I just rolled with it.

Vincent stepped around me and grabbed me from behind, pinning my arms down, I flung my head back but missed his face because he was expecting it. His teeth raked my neck, not drawing blood, but when he whispered: "You're dead." I knew he'd gotten me.

I stomped down on his foot making him bend forward and loosen enough that I was able to drop to the floor and spring away, out of his grasp. He came after me a split second later, but I had already turned and met him head to head. He took hold of my throat as I slammed the heel of my hand into his sternum. The air whooshed out of his lungs, and I pounded down on the inside of his elbow forcing his thick fingers from my jugular.

He tried to swing in behind to get me in a headlock, but I ducked down and spun out, getting behind him instead and catching him suddenly in the move he was planning to use on me. I was too light to keep him there, but I had him for a second, and if there had been a blade in my other hand, he would be without a head right now.

We flew apart, pausing for a moment to look at each other, both panting hard but smiling.

My lips moved of their own will and whispered: "You're dead."

CHAPTER FIFTEEN

"The man we are going to see is a bit eccentric," Vincent said from where he sat behind the wheel of his sporty little super-charged automobile. We sped down the freeway at about 90 mph. Vincent's lead foot had only let off when he saw what he thought was a police car. It turned out to be a van full of kids with roof racks. I only chuckled a little bit when he slowed.

His speeding would probably get his license revoked if he got caught, but I didn't tell him to slow down. The car had so much power. The freeway was nearly deserted at this time of night and with my new found love of adrenaline, I was enjoying the high speed.

"What do you mean by eccentric?" I asked.

"You will have to wait and see. There is no describing Emanuel," he laughed.

"Fun, I love surprises." I do not love surprises, and I made sure my tone conveyed that.

He turned the radio up, and we drove for almost another hour before he pulled off the highway and straight through a small town. When he turned off onto a small logging road and parked, I couldn't see a house anywhere. The dirt lane was blocked with a huge cement slab, apparently meant to keep vehicles out if they disregarded the sign that said 'no trespassing' nailed roughly to a tree.

Vincent never missed a step. He walked boldly past the barricade and up the small, overgrown lane. I hurried to catch up to him, and he slowed his pace when he realized I was, once again, jogging to keep up with his freakishly long legs.

About a half mile up the lane, there was a small clearing to the right. Vincent stopped and turned toward it.

"Good evening, Emanuel," Vincent said to the empty clearing. I took a step forward, squinting into the forest, expecting to see someone. There was no movement and no shapes in the shadows.

"Who are you talking to? There is no one there, Vincent." I spun back to look at him.

"Look again," he said, nodding his chin towards the clearing.

Before me stood a beautiful cottage with open Dutch windows above ornate cast iron flower boxes, overflowing with yellow pansies. The small porch on the front of the one-story home had a bench swing, and on that swing, rocking peacefully, was a tiny man. He wore a dark green velvet suit and top hat. The perfect picture of a leprechaun.

"Is he a lep…?" Vincent's hand covered my mouth, stopping my question.

The little green man stopped swinging. "I am an elf, I'll thank you not to compare me to those varmints," he uttered, scowling.

"Sorry, she's brand new, Emanuel. You can't blame her when you dress like the human's notion of a leprechaun. Besides, she is Durga. I thought you might like to meet her." Vincent smiled at me and nudged me forward.

I still had no idea why we were here. Vincent just said we needed to go shopping.

"You don't say," his little eyebrows shot up under the brim of his hat. "Very well, come inside. Just keep your bloody vampire fingers off my wares," said the elf as he hopped off his swing and opened the front door to the cottage.

I snorted a laugh and Vincent gave me a harsh look which only caused the laughter to bubble up harder. I managed to get myself under control as we walked into the tiny cottage and were suddenly in a giant warehouse with dozens of small men and women working. It was so hot I took off my jacket, but it was still much too hot for long pants and boots. I prayed we wouldn't have to stay long.

As we walked farther into the building, we passed people heating metals and pouring them into moulds, the sound of hammers hitting steel met my ears, and the smell of the fires singed my nose.

"You may have any you choose, but choose well, Durga, for the blade will never leave you."

"What does that mean?" I asked my attention mostly on the rows of glistening knives and swords.

"Magical weapons will always return to their owner. Once you touch one, it will be yours for life and never lost." He waved me towards the display of weapons.

Well, that sounded perfect. Weird, but perfect. I would never have to worry about misplacing it or someone taking it from me.

I strolled along the row, taking in the details of the various weapons. Some were plain, others, so ornate, they appeared to be more decorative than utilitarian.

There were easily hundreds to choose from. I had no knowledge of swords or knives beyond steak and butter knives.

I was just about to start asking questions when I saw it. The blade was no more than the length of my forearm and narrow but etched into the steel was a lark in flight. The detail was so delicate, it looked like a silver lark was flying out from within. Its wings clipped the top and bottom of the width of the blade. My hand moved of its own power and picked it up before I thought about it anymore.

"An excellent choice!" the Elf clapped his small hands, popping me from my fascination with the knife.

"Beautiful," Vincent whispered, looking me in the eye.

I had never thought of a knife as beautiful before, but this one certainly was. It fit in my hand well, but I had never used a knife as a weapon before. I wanted to set it down, unsure what to do with it, if I was holding it correctly, and afraid I would cut someone accidentally. Of course, as I set it on the table, I bumped it somehow and nicked my palm.

I hissed a breath, but my palm healed, and I wiped the blood off my hand on my jeans. The blood on the knife, however, disappeared, like the blade had soaked it up.

"Ah, good, the knife has chosen you too. Very well, take your vampire and off you go. Make the world a safer place and whatnot," he dismissed us with the wave of his hand.

Vincent walked back out the door, and I followed behind him, holding my blood sucking knife awkwardly. Isn't it just my luck that I would choose a weapon that wanted to drink my blood. Fucking vampires. I wondered if all the knives and swords the elves had made were bloodthirsty. Some weird magic.

At the car, I pulled the handle to get in the passenger seat but startled when I flipped the handle and realized it was locked.

I turned back to say something to Vincent about it, but he was right behind me. Way too close. I took a step back, bumping into the car and he took a step forward.

He wordlessly took my arm, bringing my hand with the knife up and moving my fingers until they aligned nicely on the handle of the blade. I thought he was showing me how to hold it until he then wrapped his hand around mine, tightening my grip almost painfully around the knife handle. He moved my hand until the tip of the blade pointed at his neck.

"Stop, what are you doing?" I asked him.

He ignored my words and even as I began to struggle to get my blade away from his neck, he pushed his neck onto the razor edge and drew a small cut. Blood leaked down towards the collar of his shirt.

"What is wrong with you?" I screamed, thrashing in his hold but he simply took a small step back, let go of my hand and looked at me with a resigned look on his face, saying nothing.

I shoved him and scrambled to the far side of the car. My breathing laboured, heart pounding in my chest. Durga looked out through my eyes and then slipped away again, uninterested.

After a few more moments he finally spoke.

"I always wondered if Durga would kill me if we crossed paths. Someday you might, but I suppose today is not that day." He pulled the keys out of his pocket and unlocked the doors. The sound of the locks releasing and the alarm disengaging with a beep, startled me. He began walking around the car toward the driver's side, approaching me. I circled the vehicle, keeping the car between us.

He got in the car but didn't start the engine. He looked disappointed. That I hadn't killed him? Why would I have killed him? I was missing something, as usual. I stood beside the passenger door for a long time before I finally opened the door and got in the car.

As soon as I did, Vincent started the engine and backed out onto the main road. He drove for a long time, eyes forward, no expression on his face.

When my body stopped shaking, and my heart returned to normal, I felt strong enough to speak.

"Why did you do that?" I whispered.

He swallowed, his Adam's apple bobbing in his throat. "Durga decides who should die."

I rolled the words around in my head for a few minutes. Durga decides. I'm the freaking Durga. He thought I would want him dead?

"Why would I want to kill you?" I asked, afraid of the answer.

He looked at me sadly. "Durga decides who deserves to die."

"Stop speaking in riddles, you shit head. Are you saying I don't decide?"

He shook his head. "My blood would tell you if I should die. Every time we fought, you bloodied me, but you had no means to kill me, I had to know. If I was going to die, I wanted it to be on my terms."

"Pull over," I said.

He looked at me.

"I said pull over!"

As the car rolled to a stop, I flung the door open and skidded down the ditch and lost the dinner I had eaten before we left the mansion. Some of it hit my shoes. That would never come out. That fucking vampire. He would have let me kill him right there.

Vincent and I had a rough start, but he and I had made some common ground, and I even started to think of him as a friend.

"You fucker," I yelled up to him where he stood on the side of the highway watching me.

I stomped up the ditch, wiping my mouth, wishing I had put my hair up in a ponytail. I was going to be smelling vomit all the way home.

I shoved him hard, his back hitting the car, but his hands remained at his sides.

"How dare you! You don't get to decide anything for me. I decide who I stab. It is on my terms, not yours, and I don't want you dead. I never want you dead!" I screeched the last part, making me wince a little at the sound of my own voice.

He bit his lip and nodded his head. What was wrong with him?

Fast as lightning, he grabbed me and switched our positions, pushing me against the car again. This time, I didn't have the knife in my hand, it was on the floor in the front seat of the car. When his lips met mine, I was so shocked I didn't even try to shove him away until I remembered what had just happened in that ditch and turned my head to the side, breaking the kiss.

"You idiot, I taste like vomit," I said, covering my mouth with my hand.

He just chuckled. Hearing the lightness return softened my anger. I kept my mouth covered but looked back at him as he moved back half a step. There were no street lights on this section of the freeway, but the moon was full, and I could see his expression. He looked like a man reborn. Maybe hearing that Durga didn't want him dead had given him a new lease on life. His mood sure as hell couldn't have been improved by kissing my polluted lips. I wanted to barf again at the taste in my mouth.

Vincent flashed me a toothy smile and walked around behind the car, getting into the driver's seat.

He stopped at a gas station rest stop and filled the car's gas tank. When he returned from the convenience store, he handed me a pack of gum, and I thanked God for the vampire.

Spearmint was the real hero tonight, saving me from the torture of my own mouth for the rest of the drive home.

At the mansion, Vincent stopped at the front door and turned off the car, but as I turned to get out, he stopped me.

"Please don't tell anyone what I did. I won't be able to control the vampires if they think…well, it just wouldn't be good for anyone. I will teach you how to fight with a knife starting tomorrow." He pushed some hair that had fallen forward behind my ear and ran his fingers down my cheek and kissed me gently before abruptly sliding out of the vehicle.

I shook my head and got out too, only to be greeted by a practically vibrating, angry warlock.

CHAPTER SIXTEEN

"What are you all huffy about?" I asked as I climbed the steps to the mansion.

"I don't know, Lark. Maybe the fact that I come over here to talk to you and find you kissing the asshole vampire."

I turned on him. "And where is your fiancé tonight?"

He had the decency to look ashamed but still followed me into the foyer.

He ran his hands through his hair in frustration. "Can I please talk to you?"

"You can use my office, Lark," Vincent called as he climbed the stairs towards the bedrooms.

"Come on then," I said and led the way. The warlock trailed behind me without a word, until he shut the door.

"Lark," he said, stepping into my space. "I'm sorry about Cindy. What she said is true, but I won't ever marry her. She knows that but insists on making my life miserable."

I took a step back. I had real problems to deal with, like rogue vampires and stuff. I had never had to deal with this kind of problem before. Boy problems. I had no idea how to make this all go away, and I didn't want to get close to someone and have them ripped away from me again.

Unfortunately, Frankie read that thought and responded, "I'm not going anywhere, Lark. I'll be right here."

I sighed. "Ok, well I need to get to bed, Frankie. I'm tired, and I don't know how to deal with this right now, ok?"

He nodded but didn't say anything more about it. Thank God.

I walked him back to the front door and waved goodbye. Frankie was important to me, but my life was already so complicated.

I realized I had left my knife in the car, but as soon as I thought that, the blade was in my hand. I laughed. Magic.

***

"So, did you smooth things over with your lovesick warlock?" Vincent snickered as I stabbed my plastic training knife towards his eye. Vincent was too scared to let me use my real knife for practice. At least that's what I taunted him with when he handed me this safety knife. I didn't think I would feel good about accidentally stabbing him, though. Truth be told, I wasn't sure I wanted to stab anyone with my knife, now that I had it. A little scrape or a broken nose was one thing but cutting off a vampire's head was grotesque. Thinking about it made my stomach turn.

I couldn't get the hang of stabbing. It seemed like such a simple thing, in theory, but in reality, it was a very demanding form of fighting. The stakes were higher when your opponent had a knife and the target smaller when you were trying to hurt them with yours.

The minor damage didn't even slow a vampire down. It had to be immediate, significant damage, or you would be dead before you got a second chance.

I swung my plastic knife towards Vincent's head. He blocked it and grabbed me, spinning me around into a headlock. I stabbed him in the leg, but it just slid off his pants. The bendable blade tip probably didn't even leave a bruise.

"You aren't concentrating," he whispered in my ear then spun me back around to face him, holding me at arm's length.

"I am trying, the problem is that I have a stupid plastic knife in one hand, so I can't fight you, and I'm not fast enough to stab you anywhere important," I complained.

Yes, it was the first day of trying to fight with a knife. No, I didn't think I was asking a lot of myself to be good at it. Where was Durga, anyway?

"Call your blade, Lark."

"What?"

"Call it to you."

I switched the plastic knife to my left hand and held out my right. The dazzling blade appeared there instantly. I smiled as it sparkled in the fluorescent lights of the gym then firmed up my grip.

He held out his hand, and after a moment I unhappily handed him the blade.

He cut his arm, and the scent of copper pennies filled the room. I stared at him in shock as blood dripped down his arm where it hung beside him. He was so nonchalant about hurting himself. I suppose when I got used to my healing power… Nope, I still wouldn't go around slicing and dicing myself.

He set my sharp blade down on a weight bench, and I shifted the plastic knife back into my right hand. The scent of his vampire blood dumped adrenaline into my system, and I attacked him with new found energy. My plastic knife moved more smoothly through the air and slid across his chest in an arc that would have sliced him deeply if my blade wasn't made from the same material as Gumby.

"That's better," he smiled.

I spun and made to stab him in the chest, just as he ducked away and came up behind me to try and grab me again, but I was faster than him this time and shoved my blade out just as he appeared, thrusting it directly into his neck. He made a gagging noise as the plastic jammed his windpipe. I was very thankful I wasn't holding my steel blade at that moment.

"Holy shit, you are so dead," I laughed as he coughed and cleared his throat.

"Thank you, Durga, for this lesson in humility."

I stopped laughing.

"Do you think we are two different people, Vincent?" I asked plainly. He had said something similar on the highway. That Durga decides. But, I was Durga.

"You must be."

"Why must we be?"

He considered me for a minute like he was trying to solve an advanced equation.

"It's the magic," he said, like that answered all the questions. "You smell different when you are fighting me as Durga. Lark smells like the breeze after the rain, but Durga smells like burning leaves.

Ugh. Why must he sniff me?

"Ok, well, I assure you, I am still me."

After a moment he nodded. "Alright, Lark, let's go again."

I kicked his vamp ass several more times, and he decided I was ready to get back out on the street with team Lark.

***

"Hey Lark!" the team cheered. Of course, our team had lost two members last time we were all out together, so a new vampire had been added. He joined in the cheering even though we hadn't met. Herd mentality, I guess. New guy looked like a surfer. His longer roguish blonde hair was styled to look like he just stepped out of a magazine, tanned skin and easygoing boyish smile.

"This is Drew. He was part of another team. A couple of them moved into private security, so Drew joined team Lark last week. We have just been waiting for our Lark to fly back in," Cedric said, flapping his hands like birds' wings. Idiot.

"Well, here I am. Let's go check out some smelly nightclubs and find some dirty bloodsuckers," I said.

***

It was Friday night. Ladies night, which I wouldn't have known except half-drunk men in the bar kept telling me. Like the fact it was a special night 'for ladies' made it more likely they would get lucky.

The smell of cheap beer and cheaper cologne clogged my sinuses as I made my way through the crowd to the front of the dance floor where a group of girls my age were dancing. That feeling of normalcy that I felt when surrounded by a group of giggly college girls took me over. I loved it, and kind of hated it.

A man started dancing behind me. He was cute and normal. I began to get a bit depressed. This wasn't where I was supposed to be.

I caught Cedric's eye and pointed to the door, already moving through the crowd in that direction.

Out on the street, I took a left. The rest of the team followed me as I wandered the dark city blocks looking for something. I didn't know what, but it wasn't in the bars. Cedric kept trying to get me into the nightclubs as we passed, but they didn't feel right.

There. A park. The grassy areas on the edge gave way to the dense shadows of the treed area. That was where my feet were taking me. I hopped the curb and jogged across the road, straining my ears to try and hear the slightest sound.

A muffled cry sent me racing forward, my palm itching to call my knife, but I held off.

I slid past some trees and in the pale moonlight I saw the flash of glowing eyes I had been looking for. My prey.

I stalked closer. The vampire hissed at me over the unmoving body at his feet like he was a mountain lion protecting his dinner. After a moment, he stood slowly, licking his bloodstained lips, aiming for a new victim already.

This vampire wasn't a rogue. He was a wild animal. I remembered the story of the fallen vampires. How they were insatiable. That is what this vampire had become. Part of me felt sympathy for the vampire. The other part just wanted his blood spilled on the soft grass.

When he charged me, with eyes glowing bright red, my decision was already made. My blade appeared in my hand as he reached me, his teeth aiming for my throat. I danced to the side and spun, trying to get in behind him, but he was fast and fueled by bloodlust.

He turned back to me, reaching out to try and get ahold of me, but my blade came down and sliced through his arm to the bone. He screamed in rage but didn't slow. The smell of his blood confirmed what I already knew. His time was up. Durga demanded his death. My next jab caught him in the shoulder, just shy of his throat, giving him the opportunity, he needed.

He grabbed my wrist and twisted, fracturing my arm in several places. The pain radiated, and I landed hard on my ass as he shoved me away. Jumping up before he could get the upper hand, I called my blade to my left hand. I was about to attempt another slice to his neck when Vlad appeared behind him and abruptly ended our fight by removing the vampire's head with his hands.

Blood gushed like a geyser as the body crumpled to the ground.

I lifted my shaking arm and pulled it into my chest. The vampire's death popped the happy bubble that fighting gave me and now it fucking hurt.

"Sorry, Lark. Vincent said not to let you get hurt. You will get the next one," Vlad said with a weak smile.

I turned around, dropped to my knees and vomited on the grass. Shit. I was never going to be taken seriously as Durga if I puked every time things got extra messy.

Cedric silently offered me a tiny hotel size bottle of gin. I took it and used it to rinse my mouth.

"Holy shit that was crazy cool." This came from the new guy. What was his name again? Drew. I stood up and moved away from the place I had dropped.

"I have never seen a human move that fast. I know you aren't a human, but you are fast as hell. That was insane. We have the best team ever." He held up his hand for a high five, but when I just raised my eyebrows at him, holding my broken arm to my chest, he dropped his hand and mouthed the word 'oops.'

"Chill dude," Tommy said patting the over-excited puppy on the back once as he walked by.

Tommy took out his cell, made a silent call and within moments a couple vampires appeared in the clearing and started bundling up the headless vampire.

Cedric checked the victim but shook his head at Vlad and then herded us out of the park.

A phone rang, and Tommy answered it, then handed it to me. It was awkward to hold it with my left arm, but my right wasn't entirely healed yet.

"Hello?" I said into the phone.

"Are you alright?" Vincent's voice came back down the line.

"I'm fine, Vincent," I replied. Why the hell was he calling me? And on Tommy's phone?

"Come back to the house," he said and hung up.

I handed the phone back to Tommy and reached around, awkwardly to my back pocket with my left hand and fished out my phone. The screen was shattered, and the case had cracked Ugh. All my good stuff was on that phone. As I mourned, we entered the parking garage.

The lower level we had parked on had a few lights out, so it was dim, and one bulb flickered, giving the place an eerie feel. We were walking in silence towards the van, the sound of our feet echoing through the underground structure the only sound, when suddenly my knife was in my hand. Before I had time to question its appearance, I spun and slashed my blade across the neck of a vampire who had sprung up behind me, his teeth aimed for my throat.

As he dropped, two more vampires took his place in front of me, and I realized we were under attack. There were probably ten vampires against the four of us, but I didn't feel any fear. The scent of blood from that first vamp spilled adrenaline into my veins and blocked the pain from my injured right hand. I switched my knife back to that hand and faced the rogues straight on. I saw Gabby fighting Tommy and cursed. That bitch.

My rage made me see red, and I started slicing and stabbing by instinct alone. The more blood I spilled, the more I craved. These demons were not going to hurt my team.

When there were only three rogues left, including the traitor, Gabby, they ran for it.

I was about to go after them but saw Tommy lying on the ground. He was still breathing, but his skin was pale, and a puddle of blood was quickly expanding around him.

Vlad scooped him up, and Cedric opened the van door. They slid Tommy in, and we all piled in after him.

I could see Tommy's wound closing, but he was so pale, and his breathing was ragged.

I covered my mouth as a dry heave wracked my body."

"Don't you puke in this van, Lark," Cedric ordered. I called him some choice names in my head, but I didn't dare open my mouth. I just thought of happy places and times. When that failed, I closed my eyes, slowed my breathing and dropped my hand. Thank God for meditation. I let the world slip away as my mind travelled to somewhere my body couldn't follow.

***

I was sitting in front of Shiva again. This time he was staring right back at me.

"Hello, Durga," the ancient God said. The snake around his neck hissed and coiled like it would strike. Shiva noticed my trepidation and raised his hand to the snake who just coiled around his wrist. The snake was content to play a strange game of jungle gym over the deity's body.

"My name is Lark," I replied.

"That is an unusual name. Durga does like unusual though. I'm not surprised she chose you. Where is she now?"

"What do you mean?" I asked, still keeping my eye on that snake.

"Usually she comes to me, why are you here instead?" He rolled his hand, and the snake slithered up his arm. He petted its head with his other hand and cooed at it.

I shivered at the sight. What the hell?

"I have no idea."

"Very well, you may come to me for the guidance of my will, but I am a very busy God and have much to do. Farewell," he said as he faded to black.

CHAPTER SEVENTEEN

"Come back, Lark."

I peeled my eyes open. Somehow, I was in my room in the mansion. Hadn't I been in the van? And did I talk to Shiva? That was weird. Maybe I hit my head or something. You would think the god of destruction would be more … something. All-powerful, scary, perhaps not someone who would coo at a pet snake.

"You smell like candy when you meditate," the vampire informed me.

"I told you to stop sniffing me. Gross," I moaned, rolling off my bed and staggering towards my bathroom. I stopped dead in the middle of the room when I looked at the window and realized it was daylight. What the hell?

"How long was I meditating?"

"About five hours. I was about to call your warlock to see if he had some spell to wake you." He looked at me expectantly, like I had some answer to the obvious question of what the hell had happened.

Five hours? I finished my walk to the bathroom and flicked on the shower. "I'm going get the gross off me," I said, trying to buy time to figure it out myself. I had definitely seen Shiva.

"And he is not my warlock," I said, slamming the bathroom door.

I pulled out some mouthwash and gargled liberally before spitting it in the sink. When I looked up in the mirror, my eyes flashed red for a second. What the hell was that? I remembered my vision turning red when I was in the park. Was I turning into a vampire? I stumbled back, knocking over the mouthwash and tripping on the bath mat, falling on my ass.

"Are you alright, Lark?" Vincent called from my room. Was I alright? I didn't know how to answer him. Everything was spinning. My breath came in and out in harsh puffs. The door crashed in, and suddenly a raging vampire had scooped me up.

"What is wrong?" he yelled from the smashed doorway. His booming voice snapped me back to reality.

"My eyes turned red," I said as he sat down on the edge of the bed with me. "I think I'm becoming a vampire."

He snorted and started laughing. It wasn't funny. I didn't want to drink blood. Jerk.

"You can't be a vampire, Lark. You are Durga. You will never be a vampire."

I considered his words for a minute and thought back to the photocopied information he had given me when I signed his contract.

Oh, no. He did not. I looked him in the eye and spoke very carefully.

"Do you have more information about being a Durga, Vincent?" my quiet, controlled tone knocked the humour right out of him. He didn't have to reply, I could tell from the look on his face that I had caught him red handed.

I pushed off him and stood up. Pointing my finger right in his face, I scowled and said, "You will produce all the information you have about Durga or I will kick your ass and you know I can do it, Vincent Crowden."

He stared at me for a moment and then nodded.

"Good, now, get out. I need to have a shower, and you broke my bathroom door."

He stood and left without another word.

Smart vampire.

***

Later that evening, when I woke, I found a book on my nightstand. The book was called Vampire and Durga – a history. The book was old, pages yellowed, but the type was still legible.

I sat and read. Most of it was the story of the ancient vampires. Vincent, Vlad, and a few others including Vernon, the fallen vampire that Vlad had told me about.

It said that they were all brothers. Turned into vampires and left behind by a vampire who had happened upon their settlement. The brothers didn't know what they were or why they craved blood, but their story was long. Most of the book was dedicated to their early years, figuring out who they were and what they were. Eventually, they met up with other vampires and created more of their kind. Those seemed like dark years for the brothers, filled with bloodlust.

I flipped to the middle of the book and found the story of Vincent crossing to the new world. He had run because of stories of a hunter, Durga, who was slaughtering vampires in their native country. The story told of some vampires who were spared because they were careful not to kill humans, and Vincent believed he would not be spared if he stayed. He wanted to start a new life. Vlad soon followed, but the rest of the brothers scattered to the wind.

No wonder Vincent had been so angry our first few meetings; Durga had run him from his home.

The last few pages bound in the book were a letter from Vaughn. I recognized the name from the notes I had found on Vincent's desk. The pieces clicked together. Vaughn must have been another brother. His letter included a ton of information about Durga.

Strength, top speed, abilities. They were all listed there in the form of a scientific study. The fact they couldn't be turned into a vampire. The desire to hunt their prey, the day sleeping. The Sight.

The letter also told of the story of Durga which I already knew thanks to my study of Yoga. Her name meant the inaccessible or the invincible. She was the warrior goddess of Hinduism and the slayer of demons.

Satisfied enough, I set the book down and went to start my night.

The dining room was full, but I caught a glimpse of my team on the far side of the room. I filled a plate and joined them.

"Lark!" they called as I sat down.

"You ready for another fun night of hunting, Lark?" That was Drew. He always seemed to be excited.

"Sure," I replied between mouthfuls of food.

"It's going to be awesome," he said before standing to take his dishes back to the kitchen.

"Conference room in twenty!" Cedric called. Drew waved and continued on.

"Mr. Crowden wants us to wrap up early tonight," Cedric said as he grabbed up his dishes and followed out behind Drew.

I wanted to ask him why, but he was already gone.

I turned to Vlad. "Do you know what's happening?"

He smiled. "Lark, I think it is supposed to be a surprise."

Ugh. "Oh goody. I love surprises," I said.

He laughed at my expense, then patted my shoulder and left with Tommy to return his dishes.

That night we drove around for hours, everyone in the van watching me for some sign we might be near a vampire I wanted to hunt and kill. It was pretty annoying actually, their eyes crawling all over me, so eventually, I told Cedric to park the van, so I could get out and walk.

It was several blocks later when I felt a pull, or maybe it was a push. Drew cheered when I suddenly turned, crossed the street, and hustled towards an abandoned building. From the outside, it looked vacant, but in this area of the city, a building with a solid roof and boarded up windows was never empty. It was a hub.

Inside drug addicts were shooting up, and vagrants were bedding down. The stench burned my eyes and throat, making me want to leave again, but the pressure to continue was stronger than my desire to flee.

The main floor didn't produce any sign of a vampire, so I moved to the second floor, the team close behind me.

I opened the first door to the left, but the room was empty. To the right was a pair of rooms with their doors open. The first was occupied by a naked man snoring on a mattress on the floor. Ick.

The last room was darker than the rest. The windows covered by an opaque material blocking out the small amount of light from the moon.

"I'm sorry, Durga. I didn't mean to kill that girl," a voice whispered from the darkness. "You have to believe me,"

Cedric walked in behind me to look at the man cowering in the corner. My eyes had adjusted, and I could now see the small shape of him. He was only wearing pants. His dirty bare feet trembled on the floor in time with his trembling lips. I could count his ribs and his arms, thin as sticks, were wrapped around his legs. His face was tucked into his knees, but his hair was long and dirty.

I was stunned at the sight of him. He didn't look like he could even hurt a fly, much less a person.

"Rise," I said, my lips moving against my will.

The man's sobs wracked his tiny frame as he unfolded to a height not much more than my own.

"Why does he look like that?" I asked Cedric, not taking my eyes off my prey.

"That is what a starving vampire looks like," Cedric replied in a hushed tone.

"Why are you starving?" I asked the man.

"I don't want to hurt anyone. Please, Durga!" He begged.

"How do you know I am Durga?"

"The rogues told me. They warned me the human with red eyes was going to kill me. They tried to get me to join them, to fight for them, but I don't want to hurt anyone."

"And what are the names of these rogues?" my voice was stern now. I had accepted that when Durga took the wheel my eyes were red, though it still surprised me when this small vampire mentioned it. I didn't expect it was something I would get used to.

"I don't know! Please, you have to believe me. I left, I didn't want any part of them or what they were planning."

"Come forward," my voice said.

He was shaking more violently now, his eyes still looking at the floor.

"Give me your hand, vampire." I wasn't sure what was happening right now, but I wasn't in control anymore. I felt the pressure to release control to Durga. Maybe Vincent had been right. Perhaps we were two different people. If I was about to slaughter this man, I was not looking forward to having a front row seat to it. I struggled to stop myself, but as his hand came up, I grabbed it, my knife appearing in my other hand at the same moment and slicing down his arm. The scent of his blood filled the room.

The man squeaked but didn't pull away. Like he was ready to have whatever fate I decided for him.

"You are spared," with that, my body was once again under my own power, and I dropped the vampire's hand.

"Thank you," the small man whispered before collapsing to the floor.

After a long pause of quiet, it was broken by Drew who whispered, "That was fucked up."

His words seemed to bring us all back to the present. Vlad caught the petite vampire as he passed out and carried him out the door.

I followed the team out of the house, consumed by my thoughts. Durga had taken complete control. I didn't want to cut that vampire, but she forced me. I was not ok with this arrangement.

The little vampire still hadn't woken when we arrived back at the mansion, so Drake led Vlad to a small bedroom and set up an IV of bagged blood for the starving man.

"Vincent would like to speak to you," Drake said as he put a blanket over the slight figure on the bed. He looked even smaller laid out like that. Frail. His arms and legs were mere sticks, and the blanket lay nearly flat on the bed, giving little indication that anyone lay beneath it.

I turned and left, hoping the new vampire would make it.

"Come in," Vincent said from his office when I knocked on the door.

"Hi," I said softly, sitting down on the chair in front of his desk.

He smiled and shook his head. "I hear you brought home a stray."

"He didn't deserve to die," I said sullenly.

"So, you didn't kill anyone, and that makes you unhappy?"

I snorted, "No, it's just, I think you were right. I couldn't stop myself. I tried, but I couldn't stop myself from cutting that vampire. I thought I was going to kill him, and I couldn't stop it." I pulled my feet up onto the chair and hugged my knees.

"I'm sorry, Lark."

"What are you sorry for?" I asked.

"For dragging you into this life. You probably could have kept running from it your whole life, if I hadn't pushed you so hard."

"It's not your fault. It's better, not being afraid all the time, but I don't feel in control right now. Like my old life is gone, and my new life is all about death and destruction."

He sighed then stood up. "I have something that might cheer you up."

"I doubt it."

"Don't be like that, Lark. Come on. You will love this."

I trailed behind him as we left the mansion and got in his car. He drove out, and when he stopped the car, I couldn't believe my eyes.

"It's beautiful," I gasped.

The sign on the top of the building read Sun Down Yoga in bright red letters on a yellow background in the half-circle shape of a sunset.

The front of the building had been completely redone in new vinyl siding.

Randy stood at the door, beaming, as I walked up. I hugged him and walked into my new yoga studio for the first time. I had hardly had time to eat, much less visit to see how construction was coming along the last few weeks, so I was amazed to find the whole place shone with peaceful, positive energy. My vision come to life.

The floors were an earthy bamboo wood that glowed with warmth. The walls had been painted in the soft blues and muted greens I had chosen to accent and enhance the feeling of calm and peace. One entire wall was mirrored, giving the space an open feel and the mirrors would help beginners find their body space.

I spun around, and the inside of the front wall was awash with the sunset painted by the artist I had hired. The colours made me feel like I was looking at a real sunset.

I walked into the middle of the room and sat down. It was finished. It was perfect.

"You aren't going to meditate, are you?" Vincent asked, concern lacing his voice. I still hadn't explained to him about seeing the Hindu God when I meditated. It felt too personal to share with anyone.

"No, I'm just feeling the space. It's so calm and peaceful. Thank you, Vincent."

"You don't have to thank me," he said, sitting down beside me on the floor. I laughed as he ran his hand over the floor and checked to see if it was clean. He was already sitting on it. If it had been dirty, his pants would already be ruined.

"When do you want to book your open house? We should give the newspapers a week to run some advertising and write a story.

"Why would the newspaper write a story about my yoga studio?"

"I will ask them to. I own both daily newspapers that run in this city."

"Why am I not surprised? I guess a week is fine."

He just smiled, and we sat in silence for a little while.

Eventually, I grew tired, and we stood up to go home.

I hugged Randy again. "Thank you for all your help with this."

"You got it, Lark. Would it be ok if I stayed on to run the front desk and do the books and things?"

"Absolutely," I replied. Randy was perfect for a yoga studio. He was so sweet and calm. "I don't know how I will pay you though. I might not have income for a while."

"Don't worry about that," Vincent replied. "Randy is in my employ. I can loan him to you until your business is making money and you can afford to hire him."

"Alright, as long as that's ok with you." I turned towards Vincent, but he just nodded. I remembered what Randy had said about Vincent not having work for anyone but warriors.

At least I was able to give Randy a job he seemed to enjoy. It was time for me to get back to something I enjoyed, too. Yoga was a big part of me, and maybe I had forgotten that in these last few weeks. No more. I needed to make sure I took care of myself to keep balance in my life.

At the mansion, I slipped into my yoga pants and hit the gym. Not many people were around the house, and no one was in the gym, so I plugged my old iPod into the speaker system and let the music fill the room.

I started going through some basic poses and let my breathing drop off into a steady rhythm as I moved through some more difficult positions until I had a light sheen of sweat covering my body and my lungs and heartfelt in sync. My body moved smoothly with a strength I hadn't had before. My arms didn't shake on certain poses that I had struggled with, and my feet were firmly rooted to the ground.

When I finally sat cross-legged on the floor and let my mind drift, not caring if I meditated the day away, I was comfortable in my skin and felt like I finally had the wings I hadn't known I was longing for. I felt whole, complete.

Joy had been such a foreign concept, but I got it now. This was it. My new life was taking flight.

CHAPTER

EIGHTEEN

The next week was quiet. We went out every night but didn't find any vampires. Vincent was getting concerned and voiced his frustration in unhealthy ways. Mainly yelling.

The small vampire I had saved, Trevor, was starting to come around. He was still painfully thin but was coming down to the dining room for meals and always sat with us. He had run away from foster care after his foster father beat him. He didn't know who turned him into a vampire, but he had been struggling for months not to hurt anyone and had slipped up, on the edge of death, killing a homeless girl the week before we found him. He was still beating himself up about it, but Durga forgave him, and I hoped someday he would forgive himself. I liked having him around. He was more like me than a vampire.

The night before the grand opening of Sun Down Yoga, we returned unsuccessful again, but this time I spotted a motorcycle in the driveway. Frankie was in the house. I hadn't seen him since he stopped by to declare he would 'always be there for me.' I mean, it was kind of stupid to say that and then disappear for a couple of weeks. I had sent him some text messages, and he had always replied, but it was short one-word answers, so I took the hint and left him alone.

In the foyer the sound of the men yelling was undeniable. I had heard them from the driveway, but it echoed through the halls like low rumbles of thunder.

I scurried down the hall towards Vincent's office. My team dispersed in every other direction. Chickens.

"You lost the right to care about her when you acted like an asshole and let her slip away," Vincent growled.

"That doesn't mean you have the right to make decisions for her. She is too important to risk like this," Frankie replied harshly.

Super, so they were fighting about me. Ugh. I thought about turning around and going back to my room to let them fight it out, but it could damage the house, and I liked this house.

"Shut up, you Neanderthals," I yelled as I walked into the office.

They both spun and looked at me. Their faces morphed from anger to guilt.

"What is going on?" I asked.

"Vincent is ignoring the danger he has put you in by advertising your studio opening. He painted an arrow to your back."

I snorted. "You think I don't know they might hit me there? We haven't seen a vampire in a week, Frankie. They haven't just decided to leave the city."

His mouth opened, and he gaped at me for a minute. "You want to risk all those people? You want to risk yourself?"

"Frankie," Durga took my voice turning my vision red, pushing me to him and put my hand on his arm. "I appreciate you are looking out for me, but that studio is going to be full of Vincent's vampires. If they are planning something, we got it."

"You can't be sure of that. They might have enough vampires to overwhelm you. There could be hundreds," he said, more calmly now, but still agitated.

"I can't hide away anymore Frankie. This is what I'm meant to do," Durga let me go, but I wasn't sure if I was grateful for her help diffusing the situation, or afraid of how easily she took the wheel.

He stared at me for a long minute and nodded his head, looking like he wanted to argue with me, but held himself back.

"I'll be there, Lark. I don't like this at all, but I'll be there in case you need me." He stormed out of the office and slammed the door behind him. I looked at Vincent and raised my eyebrows.

"Why do you have to rile each other up?" I asked. He gave me this innocent look, but I knew he liked getting Frankie going.

Stupid vampires and warlocks.

Later, I collapsed in my bed for another day, excited for the grand opening of Sun Down Yoga.

***

"You guys, we have to go!" I yelled in the door of the dining room. The team was eating, slowly. Very slowly. So slowly we were going to be late.

Trevor waved at me from his place beside Cedric, and I smiled at him and waved even though I was freaking out. Cedric had taken a shine to the young vampire too. I couldn't blame him, Trevor was very personable and funny.

"Lark, calm down, it doesn't take an hour to get there," Cedric, the slowpoke, said.

"It does if you guys move at the speed of glaciers!" I replied as I walked away hoping they would follow me. Vincent had set a procedure in place so that I was never alone today. All that meant was that I was being dragged down by a bunch of bloodsuckers with all the enthusiasm of a rock.

I passed Drake on the porch, climbed in the van and waited. A year later they finally filed out of the house and into the van. Cedric slid into the driver's seat. He looked at me in the rearview mirror, and I raised my eyebrows at him. He snickered and put the van in gear.

At the studio, Randy had gone all out. There were balloons and streamers everywhere and tables set up in the reception area with cheese and crackers and tasty baked goods. There was a punch bowl with glasses, and everything was clean and flawless.

There was still an hour until the doors opened but there was nothing left for me to do. My team and a few other vampire teams were milling about, but I told them not to touch the snacks till the doors opened.

Randy was beaming and hugged me tightly before hustling off with a dust cloth to polish something that was most likely already clean.

Frankie walked in with about a dozen warlocks and witches in tow, including everyone's favourite witch, Cindy.

I narrowed my eyes at him, as he walked towards me. "I'm sorry, I just wanted the strongest here with me." I wasn't happy, but as long as the witch didn't ruin my great day, I wouldn't have to slice her up.

Frankie laughed and squeezed my hand. "I already warned her I would make her hair fall out if she ruined this for you." Mollified at least a bit, I gave him a weak smile.

"So, what do you think of my studio?" I asked him, turning us around to look at the open area beyond the reception.

"This is amazing, Lark. It's exactly how you pictured it."

"You saw it in my mind? When?" I asked. I couldn't remember thinking about it when he was around.

"It was about eight months ago." He pulled me into the middle of the room and wrapped his arms around my waist, standing behind me and looking over my shoulder at our reflection in the mirror.

"You were drunk, and some idiot was bothering you at the bar. I was about to tell him to fuck off when your mind drifted away. It was like you were standing right here, looking around. I had no idea if it was a real place or imagined. Now I know."

I was stunned. I had never thought too hard about how much Frankie could see in my thoughts, but to see this place long before I even thought it could be a possibility was amazing. Also, heartbreaking. He lived this dream with me, and now we were standing right where I imagined I might be someday. A tear fell from my eye. The distance that had grown between Frankie and me over the last few weeks snapped up like it was never there. I was already emotional about the studio dream coming true, but to know that I had shared it with Frankie all that time ago, pushed me over the edge.

"I'm sorry," he whispered. "For being gone; For letting go when I should have held on. For not being there when I said I would."

I wiped my eyes with my hand, and he spun me around to face him, wrapping his arms around my shoulders and holding me close. I saw Vincent over Frankie's shoulder. His scowl made me feel guilty. Super, no avoiding boy drama. Frankie let me go and turned to the vampire. I needed to get better control of my thoughts.

"Truce time, vampire," Frankie said, shocking the hell out of me. He walked over with his hand extended and stopped in front of Vincent. They both just looked at each other for a moment before shaking hands and walking back out into the reception area. Leaving me alone in the studio.

When the doors opened, I was surprised to see some of my old students. A few of the elderly couples came, and one of the sweet little old ladies patted my cheek and told me how proud she was of me. The coach of one of the junior hockey teams had sent his whole team down to sign up. Randy was kept busy putting out more snack trays after the horde of teenagers left.

Several stylish looking PTA moms with kids came in and signed up, and some new moms with babies joined my mom and tot program.

It had been more successful than I could have hoped for. I was just about the shut the front door when my old yoga instructor, Shanti, walked in. I hugged her, and she had a look around.

"This is amazing, Lark!" she said as I showed her around.

"Thanks, I'm looking forward to starting classes in two weeks."

"I'm so happy for you." She hugged me, and we walked towards the door. "Why don't we meet for coffee next week? I'd love to keep in touch with you."

"Thank sounds great," I replied and gave her my new cell number before she left.

I flicked the lock on the door and went to help clean up. I had lots of people signed up for classes so I would have to start scheduling my time better; No more staying out till daybreak.

When everything was put away, and the balloons and streamers were taken down, I said goodbye and thanked Frankie for setting everything up. We all piled back into our vehicles and headed for home.

As our van approached the gate, I could see Vincent's car, and the SUV that was travelling ahead of us pull over, blocking the driveway where the gate used to stand. The gate had been destroyed. Peeled back from the posts like they had been made of paper. Everyone in the first two cars got out and started running for the house.

I reached for the door handle, but Vlad stopped me.

"We wait," he said.

I waited for a few moments and then dove for the door and slid out before Vlad could stop me. The smell of blood lingered on the air. Human blood. I raced towards the mansion. Up the long driveway, praying I wasn't going to see what I feared.

At the bottom of the steps, at the front of the mansion, in a crumpled heap, lay Drake. Vincent was crouched beside him, sorrow splashed across his face, betraying his heartbreak before it was replaced by something much more worrying. Anger. Vincent's anger could be seen from outer space. It was so intense. We all knew who had been here and done this. While all the rest of the vamps had been out protecting me, none had been left behind. Except for one.

I flew through the house, shouldered the door open and was greeted by the smell of vampire blood. Trevor lay on the floor in a pool of it, and his chest was shredded like someone had dragged him over a cheese grater exposing the bone beneath. His body was twisted, his limbs at odd angles but his torso still rose and fell lightly.

"Vlad!" I yelled down the hall. "Somebody, come quick!"

I fell beside his small form and saw his lips moving silently. I felt Durga shift inside me and slowly began to hear the harsh whisper.

"They said you are next," he rasped, then closed his eyes. I held my breath a moment, but his chest continued to rise and fall slowly. He was still alive, for now.

Cedric came through the doors and stopped dead. He must have noticed Trevor's chest still moving too because he scooped him up and I trailed them down to the medical room.

Vlad entered the house as we passed the foyer. He followed us in and set to work hooking up a new IV for Trevor, but his silence betrayed his pain at the loss of Drake.

In the confusion, Durga finally got the foothold she wanted and pushed forward.

"He was ours! Innocent!" she yelled. She and I were on the same page this time. Killing Drake was low and so was hurting Trevor. They were weak and helpless. There must be justice.

Back in the foyer, Vincent caught me as I was heading back out the door.

"No, Lark. Wait. They want you to go out and look for them alone." I kicked and shoved to get him to let me go. "This wasn't the worst of their plan, and you know it." I clawed at his arms and pounded my heels into his knees. "This was to try and make us act irrationally."

"Well, it worked," I screamed before going limp in his arms. Durga was backing down instead of rising up to fight him off.

"Drake was a good person, and Trevor was still too weak to put up a fight," I sobbed. "I shouldn't have left them here unprotected. This was the biggest mistake. It's all my fault!"

"No, it's most certainly not your fault, Lark. We all thought they would be safer here. We will get them, be patient." Vincent scooped me up in his arms and carried me into his office, setting me down on the small couch and crouching in front of me. He brushed the hair back from my face and looked me in the eye. "I'm going to make a phone call, Lark. Just stay here."

I didn't even want to go anymore. I was shaking and feeling sick now that the adrenaline was washing out of my blood. I just wanted to sleep or puke or something.

If only I had insisted on bringing Trevor and Drake. Trevor was too thin to travel. He had been gaining slowly, but it was a long road to recovery after the neglect he had suffered, and we all agreed his skeletal frame wouldn't support him for the whole open house. Drake didn't want to leave him alone.

Cedric walked into the office and informed Vincent that the rest of the house was clear. He took one look at me and pulled a small garbage can out from beside Vincent's desk and set it on the floor in front of me without a word. Stupid vampire thinks he knows me so well. Ok, fine, I was feeling nauseated and all clammy.

Vincent made a quick phone call and when he hung up, looked at me. "I have back up on the way. We will get them, Lark. Give me two days

"Fine, you have two days, then Durga and I are going hunting." My blade flashed into my hand.

We   were   ready.

CHAPTER NINETEEN

That night the house mourned. Drake had been in the house for three decades, and everyone loved him. He wasn't a warrior or a vampire, but he was a valued part of the house family. His devotion to the vampires was unquestioned.

"He helped me when I became a vampire," Tommy said, standing at the front of the room. "He made sure I knew that I was still the same person; had the same morals. He was a man of few words, but when he spoke everyone listened. We are all going to miss him."

Every vampire in the room nodded and whispered their agreement.

The mood of the house was the lowest I had ever seen it. Vincent had been in his office on the phone most of the night, but he had come down to the conference room for Drakes eulogy. I was told they don't usually have a funeral for their dead. We hadn't had one for Eric when he died, but since

Drake was a human who dedicated his life to serving vampires, they were going to honour him the way humans did.

When everyone had spoken their piece, we moved to the dining room and had a meal together in remembrance of Drake. Some of the stories circulating were funny; some were heartfelt and some probably not suitable for a funeral. It seemed Drake was a bit of a wild man in his twenties.

I wondered who would speak of me when I died and what they would say.

Death always brings up my dark past and the pain of losing my parents.

After dinner, I walked the halls for a while and then stopped at Trevor's room. He was alive. That counted for something, but his progress had been set back. It was strange that the vampire couldn't just heal himself, but it seemed that starvation had a long-lasting impact on them, making them slow to recover and weak for months, sometimes years, according to Vincent.

Trevor was sitting propped up on his bed when I opened his door after hearing his soft, "Come in."

"How are you feeling?" I asked him, sitting in the chair beside his bed that had been occupied by Cedric every other time I stopped by in the last twelve hours. Trevor and Cedric often watched TV together or played card games during the day while I slept before the rogues came, now they seemed inseparable.

"Hi Lark," he smiled weakly. "I'm fine." He was not fine. He was healing as slowly as a human. Vlad said he might even need antibiotics if he didn't heal fast enough. I smiled anyway like I was glad to hear he was 'fine.'

"That's good. Where is Cedric?"

"He went to check in with Vincent. I'm sure he will be back." He paused for a moment and bit his lip. "He keeps saying that someday I'll be a warrior because I'm such a fighter, but I don't feel strong at all, Lark. I feel weaker than when you saved me."

Now the truth came out. "I know, but you will recover from this. I think you will be a great warrior someday too." I was getting emotional sitting here with the brave little vampire. He was so sweet and human. Durga pushed forward, squashing my sadness and replacing it with anger.

"I should go. I have some work to do. You take it easy, ok?"

"Thanks, Lark."

I squeezed his hand and walked out before Durga was able to take over. I wasn't sure how much longer she would let me wait. It had only been 12 hours, and already Durga was restless. I needed to decide. Wait, or go.

I went back to my room and sat cross-legged on the floor. I was frustrated with waiting, and the itch under my skin was getting worse. I hoped meditation would help and if I happened to come across a certain Hindu God while I was meditating, maybe he would have some advice. I pulled in a deep breath and let it out slowly and set my posture, my hands on my knees, fingers and thumbs touching. I grounded myself in the moment, forgetting about the vampires and the rogues. I drifted.

***

"Why have you come back? I am very busy," said the God of Destruction as he ran his hand over the snake that was climbing up his head. I had no idea what he could be doing that he was so busy, but I do not know the business of Gods.

"Shiva, sir, uhm, I guess I just wanted to find out if I'm supposed to be waiting or if I should be out hunting."

"Hmm," he pondered as the snake went down his arm and wrapped playfully around his wrist with a flick of its tail. My full attention was on the gross snake, and I shivered.

"I suppose it would be best to have assistance, on this occasion. I assume that is why Durga waits."

"She is still pushing on me though."

"If she wanted you to go, you would already be gone. Now, good day young Meadowlark."

***

"Vincent, come on. I can't just keep sitting around here waiting. Durga is restless. We should be out looking for the rogues who did this and cleaning up the city." My skin was crawling. I was sitting on the stupid tiny couch in his office while he looked over some papers. I had already paced around and checked out a bunch of his boring books and peered over his shoulder until he told me to sit down or he would break my legs. I didn't think he was serious, but I hadn't tried sitting down for a few minutes. It wasn't helping either.

"Calm down, Lark."

I scowled at him and then slid off the couch onto the floor. It was cold and comfortable. Ok, not comfortable, but no less comfortable than the bugs crawling under my skin.

A knock at the door made me pause in my squirming.

Vincent stood up and walked to the front of his desk and then leaned back and crossed his arms. "Come," he said, the smirk on his face made me raise an eyebrow.

The door opened, and the spitting image of Vincent walked through. I looked at him and back to Vincent and back to the man who entered.

"Hello brother," Vincent said. They looked like more than brothers. They looked like twins.

"Vincent. I hear you are having some problems," the man said. His eyes drifted to me, still on the floor of the office, and he smiled, revealing his rows of sharp teeth. "Who have you got here?" the man laughed, still staring at me. I got up and dusted myself off. Ok, great first impression, Lark. Whatever.

"Vaughn, this is Lark. Lark, Vaughn, my younger brother."

Vaughn extended his hand to me. "Much younger."

"By two minutes," Vincent chimed in as Vaughn took my hand and then brought it up to his lips and kissed my knuckles.

"So, you are the new Durga. It's a pleasure to meet you, Lark."

"Thanks," I said, still stunned by the resemblance.

He chuckled and turned back to his brother.

"I brought two teams. I hope that is enough. Have you found them yet?"

Vincent cleared his throat and turned on business mode. "No, we've been staying in. I want to have as many teams on the streets as possible. I'm guessing they have twenty or more rogues now. It's not safe to send out single teams. We can combine teams and send out everyone. I'd like no less than eight per team."

I was bouncing on my toes now, ready to go.

Vaughn chuckled again when he looked over his shoulder and saw me. "She was the same way."

"Who?"

"I knew a Durga once. The woman was younger than you when she came into her powers, but she said bugs crawled on her skin when she had to go hunt."

"Ya, it's not cool, can we go? Please?"

"Why don't you go meet the teams in the conference room and we will be down soon to address everyone," Vincent replied.

"Fine." I walked out of the office and slammed the door harder than necessary. Whatever. This waiting was going to make me crazy.

In the conference room, every vampire on the property was mulling about. They were chatting and introducing themselves to the new vampires that I assumed had come with Vaughn.

"Lark!" Drew called from the other side of the room, and everyone immediately stopped talking and turned to look at me. I waved awkwardly and shuffled through the vampires to my team. The new vampires all whispered, but I heard the word Durga a couple of times. I guess news had travelled. Gossipy vampires.

"Thanks, Drew," I scowled as I stopped beside the loud mouth.

"Sorry Lark," he replied.

"It's fine. They will probably get introductions when Vincent and Vaughn come down. Did you guys know they are twins?"

Vlad chuckled. "I obviously did, but they so rarely get together, I bet most vampires have no idea."

"That's crazy, I've been here for a long time and didn't know," Cedric said, proving Vlad's point.

Just then, the vampires in question arrived in the conference room, and we all turned to listen.

"Good evening. I would like first to welcome the vampires who have come to help us take out a dangerous threat here in our country. Your assistance is appreciated. I expect all my vampires to make them feel welcome. You are all going out tonight to hunt for a pack of rogues. We believe there could be upwards of twenty in the group, so it is imperative everyone is on their toes. Do not get cornered by them."

"You will be divided up among the teams already in place," Vaughn said to his vampires. "I would like two each per American team. Jones, you will also go with Durga since we have an uneven number."

Vaughn looked to Vincent who nodded his approval.

"Very well, please see Vlad for your assigned grid area. Do not stray from your section of the city unless another team needs help," Vincent finished.

It was bizarre to hear them speak. Vincent had worked hard to lose the accent that Vaughn and Vlad shared. Vaughn seemed maybe a bit easier going and quick to smile, but otherwise, there was little to tell them apart.

Vlad handed out the grid area for each team, and we all walked to the garage and loaded up, heading out in different directions at the end of the driveway.

Our team had three extras, so we were squished in, but it didn't matter. I was finally going hunting. Durga was doing a happy dance on my insides. Psycho.

"Where to, Lark?" Drew asked from the back seat. I had wedged in the middle with Vlad, while the Romanian team leader took shotgun, but Vlad didn't seem to mind. Drew was stuffed between two giant Romanian vamps in the back seat. I tried to control my laughter when I saw the beach bum wedged in there.

"I'm not feeling anything, Drew. I'll let you know if I do," I replied.

We circled our corner of the city, Drew harassing me every few minutes like an impatient child on a road trip. I told Cedric to park when I couldn't take it anymore. Sitting still was not Durga's strong suit, and she was so close to the surface that I wasn't sure which one of us was in control. No wonder my body took over and locked her out when I meditated.

My feet hit the pavement hard and kept moving. The vampires kept up to make sure they didn't lose me, but I was nearly running. I tried to steady my breathing but was fighting a losing battle. If I didn't find a rogue soon, I was going to lose my mind.

A half hour of walking later, I felt a tug. It was pulling me down an alley, so I let it take me. My blade appeared in my hand, telling me I had finally found a target for my rage and bloodlust.

"We go in first," the giant Romanian said with his massive mitt on my shoulder, holding me in place.

Before I could even think to react, my knife was at his throat. "It's mine," said my voice.

The Romanian vamp backed off and let me lead through the door.

It was nearly pitch black, but I shuffled in and was confronted with a large living area with four couches facing a TV. Durga's senses could smell the vampires that had once been here, but they were gone now.

The vampires went through the building and cleared all the rooms. The place was empty. It was a dead end, but it confirmed the idea that many vampires were living together.

Back out on the street, Vlad took a phone call. My hearing may have improved, but I still couldn't hear what was said on the other side of the phone call.

"We have to go back to the house," Vlad said, looking at me. I knew something had happened. Turning on my heel, I led us back to the van. I wanted to stop and ask Vlad what it was, but I could feel it in my bones. I had to get back there. Now.

Cedric drove fast, but we weren't the first team back, the driveway had three other vans already, and there were a bunch of motorcycles in the yard too.

I took the front steps two at a time and tried not to wince when Drake wasn't at the door.

I heard talking down the hall that led to Vincent's office, so I went that way. There was a crowd of witches and warlocks spilling out the door.

I pushed through and entered the office. "Lark," Vincent said. Coming over and resting his hand on my cheek. He had this look like he was worried about me. I was fine.

"What happened?" I asked looking around for Frankie, "Where is Frankie?"

Cindy handed me a letter. Scribbled in black marker, it said 'Bring us Durga, and we will give you the warlock.'

I narrowed my eyes at Cindy.

"What? I just brought it to you. I'm not saying we should hand you over. I'm just delivering the message."

I turned back to Vincent. "How could they take him? He is stronger than a bunch of vampires."

"A powerful vampire could block his telepathy, and if they knocked him out before he could call magic, they could, in theory, capture him."

"Trace his phone," I said, starting to panic.

"We did and found his motorcycle in a parking garage downtown," Cindy replied. "His phone was with it."

"What the fuck was he doing there?" I yelled, getting mad.

The vampires in the room had the sense to back up, but Cindy didn't until she noticed my knife had appeared in my hand.

Then she took a few big steps back and said: "He has been trying to find the rogues. I'm not the target here, Durga."

"Bitch," I muttered as I turned and stormed out of the office. Durga may have control, but we were on the same page. The hallways cleared as I marched down them. Vampires hustled out of the way when they saw my red eyes.

My pulse was beating so hard I could hear it in my ears. The rogues had gone too far.

In my room, I sat down on the floor and crossed my legs. I needed to calm down, or I would blow up the house.

I shut my eyes and tried to calm my breathing. It was ragged and harsh for several minutes before I got ahold of it and started to bring it back down.

I let my mind blank. I wasn't sure if I would get to Shiva or not, but I needed help.

***

"You were just here," was all Shiva said as he stroked the snake that was draped around his shoulders.

"I need to find Frankie. I need your help." I kept my eye on the snake as it rose and looked me in the eye. It was much closer to me than usual. Its tongue was poking out and then sliding back in its scaly mouth only to poke back out quickly.

"Awe, he likes you. Do you want to pet him?"

Ugh. No. I did not want to pet the dark god's snake.

"No, thank you. Maybe some other time." I leaned away from the serpent, and it recoiled, wrapping swiftly around the deity's neck.

"Very well. You already have the power to find your friend. Just focus, Lark. Goodbye."

***

My eyes opened, and I closed them again, focusing as he had instructed. I slowed my breathing, and as it slowed, my senses became more focused. The scents of my soaps and shampoos in the bathroom beside me, the feel of the hard floor beneath me, the light rustle of my hair caught in the breeze of the open window. Suddenly, my senses went beyond that, and I could feel the vampires in the house. All of them. I knew exactly where they were and what they were doing,

I moved my senses out of the house. Pushing against the walls until a bubble burst in my head. I found the vampire who worked in the garage and kept the vehicles in good working order. I found a vampire in the yard, the gardener, trimming the hedges. I felt the vampire at the gatehouse. He was playing a game on his phone.

I took another deep breath. Encouraged by my success and let my mind drift some more. I felt the vampires in the van that had been out hunting and were now two blocks away, on their way back to the house. They were disappointed they hadn't found any rogues and worried about the reason they had been called back home.

I found a vampire at Arnie's. I didn't recognize him, but Durga didn't care about him, so neither did I.

I stretched my senses as far as they would go and finally felt it. Like a tickle at my consciousness, they were so far away, but every single one of them made Durga's blood boil. There were at least thirty vampires in a warehouse tucked away from the docks, in a fenced and secured area.

And every single one of them had to die.

CHAPTER TWENTY

"Quiet, Everyone." Vincent's authoritative voice cut through the chatter and all the vampires, witches, and warlocks that crowded the room turned and faced him.

"Thank you. Now, you all know your objectives. Everyone will be in position by dusk. No vehicles within five miles of the site, so we don't tip them off.

"The witch had been in contact with the vampire who has taken up a leadership role within the rogues, and they believe that Lark will be there at midnight to exchange herself for Frankie. We move in at 11 pm. Go."

With that final word, everyone began moving towards the door. The plan was simple. We would all leave the house by various means and as covertly as possible so as not to alert anyone who might be watching the house. I told him I would know if a vampire was hanging around. Now that Durga and I had found a way to stretch our powers, I could sense vampires through the whole city.

While we were coming up with our plan, Vincent pointed out that vampires often had a human around willing to help. Humans were ridiculous. Hanging out with bloodthirsty monsters of their own free will. We decided, in case humans were watching the house, we couldn't all go storming out the front gate.

The house mechanic was taking a few vans out and parking them in another mechanic's garage a few blocks over. He frequently used the shop for maintenance, so we hoped it wouldn't be suspicious. The vans, however, would be packed full of vampires, hidden on the floors.

That left only a dozen or so people to take the bus to the location. Because the house backed onto a woodlot that was only accessible by way of the gated homes that surrounded it, most of us would be leaving through the woods and coming out on the other side. We would use the backyard of a lawyer who was currently travelling with his family and wouldn't notice us trespassing. I was part of that group and would manage the team taking the bus since I was familiar with the routes already.

I walked out the back door of the house followed by a mixed group of warlocks, witches, and vampires. As we crossed the backyard, Vincent sidled up beside me.

"What are you doing here?" I asked him. Vincent had never gone out at night since I'd known him. He had said once that someone had to keep the pieces in motion and that task fell to him.

"I will be guarding you tonight, so you don't go running off and try to get yourself killed."

Bossy vamp.

"Fine, but don't get in my way. Whoever took Frankie is mine." I scowled at him. "And anyone else Durga chooses, belongs to us too," I say to appease my alter ego.

My nerves were jangling. I didn't want to be the reason all these people were killed tonight.

At the tree line, we moved together to form a line through the small wooded area. There weren't any paths through the woodlot, so it was nearly thirty feet of thorny underbrush before the scrub gave way to mossy loam and large tree trunks.

The moon was bright, but very little of its light made it through the dense canopy of the trees. My night vision had improved to the point that I could still travel through without tripping on exposed roots or rocks, and we waded through the underbrush on the opposite side of the trees, coming out, as planned, in the lawyer's yard.

A motion light kicked on, and we got a glimpse of his manicured and landscaped yard and in-ground pool. His house was set back from the road, like Vincent's, so we walked out his driveway. He had a gate, but it was low and mainly decorative, so we all just hopped it and continued to the bus stop.

This many people at a smaller bus stop would attract attention, so we spread out a bit and walked through the neighbourhood to the larger bus terminal. It was out of our way, but our group wouldn't raise suspicion there, and we left enough time to make it by bus.

Two transfers and a few odd looks later, our last bus let us off about four blocks from the warehouse. The driver raised his brows as we disembarked. He was letting us all off in the middle of nowhere. Even I had been surprised by the bus route when I looked it up online. There was no way we were catching a bus home again from here. It was the last stop on the run for the night. Hopefully, we wouldn't need to sneak home again. The plan was to have Frankie back, and the rogue's dead.

Durga stretched beneath my skin making me shiver.

Vincent noticed, of course. "You alright?" he asked. We walked the last few blocks to the warehouse. It was chilly out, but not cold.

"I'm fine, Durga is waking up. Apparently, our plan was boring, so she took a nap."

He chuckled. "It's nice to see you accepting her and your calling." Ugh, my calling. I could hear my bed calling me.

"I guess so. I mean, I can't exactly leave Frankie with these assholes."

Vincent nodded. He and Frankie hadn't gotten along at all, but I think even he wasn't willing to let the rogue vampires have him.

We crept up the last mile to the warehouse. Durga was bouncing against my insides. Scratching to get free and seek her vengeance. Whoever cursed me with this was going to pay if I got my hands on them.

My blade popped up again in my hand, but we had twenty minutes to wait, so we hunkered down in the brush along the side of the road, within sight of the warehouse.

The vans would go blasting through the gates once we were in place to cause a distraction, but we didn't want to be there too soon and risk someone stumbling upon us at the back of the warehouse.

With only 5 minutes to spare, we crept along the fence line to the back of the facility. The chain link fence was no big deal. One of the Romanian vamps silently pulled it up, and we crawled under. Dodging the security light at the back of the building, we lined up along the wall on either side of the steel door. Ready to bust some vamps.

Durga was shoving hard, so I let her take over.

Vincent whispered "Go," from right beside me and all hell broke loose.

We heard the first van slam through the front gates and scream to a stop at the front of the building. The Romanian vampire slammed into the steel door, knocking it off its hinges onto the floor and we flooded the warehouse.

The fighting began as soon as we entered. Rogue vampires came at us from all sides, knives flashing, and teeth bared.

My vision turned red as Durga took control and I clambered to get past all the idiots blocking my path. Adrenaline and Durga pushed my body to its limit as I finally got to the front line and began to fight.

My knife was bloody in moments, and I took the vamp in front of me to the ground, slicing across his neck with the precision only Durga could manage. I was along for the ride, but this time I was ready to let her have her way. I wanted Frankie back and these monsters out of our lives for good.

Another vamp took the place of the first one. This one had a longer blade than mine and a much longer reach. I stepped back as he swung but not far enough, and he nicked my arm. I hissed and lunged as his swing completed, leaving him open. My blade slid deep into his throat, and as he dropped, my knife slipping free.

A vampire stormed towards me from the side, and I spun, bringing my blade towards his throat, but he dodged in time and made a run for the door we had come in. The rest of the team was still spread out fighting monsters, leaving a straight escape for the beast. Durga said he had to die and threw my knife hard. It whistled past the fighters and embedded itself in the back of the fleeing vamp's neck. No mercy.

I turned to see someone tied to a chair in the middle of the room. Their head was down, and they had so much blood on them I couldn't tell for sure it was Frankie. I opened my hand and called the knife back to me as I started forward.

"No," screamed a familiar voice. Gabby ran towards me with her teeth bared and eyes blazing. She pulled out a gun and raised it.

I watched her, as if it was in slow motion, pull the trigger and a flash blinded me in the darkened room, but a body spun in front of me, taking my bullets. As the body blocking me fell, Gabby reappeared in my line of vision, and I watched as Vlad stepped in behind her. His hands went to either side of her head and with a quick twist, relieved her of it, letting her body crumple to the ground before discarding her head with the rest of her.

At my feet, Vincent rolled on to his back and looked up at me. Red bloomed on his white tailored shirt like morbid polka dots.

"You idiot, you could be dead right now."

He grinned at me, flashing his vampire teeth and stood up, dusting off his pants. The momentary break in the action didn't last. A bloodthirsty vampire launched himself towards me just as two more attacked Vincent. Vlad helped Vincent, and I turned my full attention to the drooling bloodsucker aiming for my throat. My blade came up and caught him under the chin, but it wasn't close enough to his neck to slow him down. We were getting closer to the man tied to the chair in the middle of the room. And when I finally got my knife into the vampire's throat, and he collapsed to the floor, I just kept going straight towards who I assumed was Frankie.

I saw Cedric come up the stairs from the lower level out of the corner of my eyes and just as I stepped up to Frankie, I heard him yell "Lark, no!" but it was too late. I felt the floor under my boot click, Durga flashed angrily in my mind, and the room exploded in light throwing me high and far, and then there was nothing.

***

I felt a sharp nudge on my kidney.
Leave me alone, Durga.

There was another nudge, this time it felt more like a kick to my kidney.

"Pushy fucking Goddess," I grumbled to my idiot alter ego as I forced my eyes open for a second before slamming them shut to save my retinas from the one million-megawatt bulb over my head.

"Oh, Yeah! Gets blown up – doesn't die. Durga for the win!"

That was Drew. I'd recognize his enthusiastic and highly unnecessary play by play anywhere. It was just idiotic.

Someone was poking at my left arm which I suddenly noticed felt like it was on fire. My blade came into my right hand from wherever it had been thrown too when I was blown up. Oh Ya. I was definitely blown up. That sucked.

"Do not stab me while I'm trying to heal you, Lark," Vincent's stern voice came from really close to the throbbing arm.

Oh gross, was he licking me again? Was that necessary? I thought I healed just fine on my own now.

"You are just too damaged to heal completely. He's helping, Lark." My eyes flew open again, and I turned towards the mind reading bastard who should be dead. "Can't kill me so easily," he said to that unspoken thought.

He had been in the center of the blast. He should be gross mush on the walls of the warehouse now.

"As lovely as that visual is," he paused. "Cindy, set protection around me when the bomb went off."

I was not touching that with a ten-foot pole. I turned my head to try and escape the uncomfortableness of that conversation and got an eyeful of the vampire licking my arm. The bone was still protruding from the skin, and the vampire's tongue was smoothing over it in long strokes. His eyes were blazing red.

"I'm going to puke," I muttered, dropping my blade to the floor with a clatter and covering my mouth. Thankfully Cedric had already planned for this eventuality and had a small garbage pail in his hand which he hastily pushed towards me as I sat up.

When I was done destroying any badass image I had ever constructed, Frankie handed me a bottle of water. My arm was almost healed. I dry heaved a few times when the bone snapped back into alignment and then felt the tight pull of the skin closing. Good as new.

"We need to talk about Vernon," Vaughn said from the doorway.

"Not now," Vincent retorted, standing to his full height which towered over me where I still lay.

"Yes, now, Vincent."

"What about Vernon?" I asked still resting uncomfortably between the vampires.

Vincent sighed. "We caught his smell in the warehouse. He wasn't there, but he had been in the last 24 hours."

"Oh, that is not good," I whispered. If that monster was in my city, we had a huge problem. "Do you think he was organizing the rogues?"

"If he was, he won't stop," Vaughn said before he turned on his heel and walked out.

Great, looks like my work wasn't done.

THE   END

Printed in Great Britain
by Amazon